"I'm sorry I threw and kicked the books."

"Apology accepted." Emily felt the strongest urge to reach out and give Landon a hug. He was still just a little boy, really. "We can meet another day to talk about reading."

He nodded, looking down at the floor.

She looked up at Dev. "And maybe you and I should have a talk soon, too," she said.

He rubbed the back of his neck. "Sure," he said. "Sometime." And then he and Landon hurried out of the library.

Don't get involved. They're not your responsibility outside of school hours.

Yet she had to admit she was curious about the father-son pair. Drawn to them, even. Rudeness and all.

A better teacher would stay objective, focused on academics, and let the school counselors handle the emotions.

But there was something about the pair that kept plucking at her, drawing her in, making her care.

All the more reason to keep them at a distance so she didn't start hoping for things she didn't deserve and couldn't have.

Lee Tobin McClain is the *New York Times* bestselling author of emotional small-town romances featuring flawed characters who find healing through friendship, faith and family. Lee grew up in Ohio and now lives in Western Pennsylvania, where she enjoys hiking with her goofy goldendoodle, visiting writer friends and admiring her daughter's mastery of the latest TikTok dances. Learn more about her books at www.leetobinmcclain.com.

Visit the Author Profile page at LoveInspired.com for more titles.

Her Easter Prayer

Lee Tobin McClain

LOVE INSPIRED
INSPIRATIONAL ROMANCE

LOVE INSPIRED®
INSPIRATIONAL ROMANCE

Recycling programs
for this product may
not exist in your area.

ISBN-13: 978-1-335-56762-8

Her Easter Prayer

This edition published by arrangement with Harlequin Books S.A.

For questions and comments about the quality of this book, please contact us
at CustomerService@Harlequin.com.

Love Inspired
22 Adelaide St. West, 41st Floor
Toronto, Ontario M5H 4E3, Canada
www.LoveInspired.com

Printed in U.S.A.

Weeping may endure for a night,
but joy cometh in the morning.
—*Psalm* 30:5

Dedicated to my sister, who teaches
adult GED students with sensible good humor
and no expectation of applause.
Thank you for all you do, Sue Spore!

Chapter One

He was watching her and the students again.

Emily Carver deliberately looked away from the dark-eyed handyman who kept finding things to repair in her library's teaching space. There had been a time, in her carefree twenties, when she'd have smiled at a handsome man who seemed to take an interest in her, but not anymore.

Anyway, his expression wasn't flirtatious so much as curious, watchful, assessing. Well. If he had a problem with the way she conducted her reading class—or the scars on her arms—so be it. She had to shepherd nine students on to their lunch hour, a task sometimes easier said than done with this particular group.

The Bright Tomorrows Residential Academy wasn't fancy, but most classrooms featured views of the Colorado Rocky Mountains.

In early April, they were a marvel of snowfields and evergreen forests and giant boulder peaks, reaching toward a sky as blue as a baby's eyes. Emily had only to glance out a window to remind herself that God's creation was far bigger than her human-size problems.

She put on a smile—easy enough when she looked at her beloved students. "Angus, remember to keep your hands to yourself," she said to a fifth grader who was pestering the boy in front of him. "Shane, you forgot your book. It's fine, here you go," she added, handing the child his copy of *The Secret Garden*. Shane tended to burst into tears at the smallest provocation.

Something Emily understood quite well. She'd been there.

Automatically she reached for Lady, but her service dog wasn't by her side. She looked back and saw her new student, Landon McCarthy, kneeling beside Lady, rubbing the shaggy poodle mix's cream-colored head.

She double-checked that the rest of her students were under the care of the lunch aide and noticed that the hyper-observant handyman had left the library, not that she was all that interested, no way. And then she walked back to Landon. The boy hadn't spoken during their reading class, but that was normal for new kids at Bright Tomorrows Academy. And if petting a service dog was his worst problem…

She reached the pair. "Landon, I didn't get the chance to tell you before class, but service dogs shouldn't be petted or touched while they're…" She trailed off and stared at the bright blue circles around Lady's eyes. "What are you *doing*? Give me that marker right now!"

He didn't, so she reached out and pulled it from his fingers. "Lady. Down." She pointed at a spot on the floor well away from the boy. "Landon, wait right here while I make sure she's okay."

"I didn't hurt her." The boy's tone was gruff.

A quick check of the dog assured her that he was telling the truth, although… She looked down at the marker. Sure enough, it was permanent.

Even if Emily was able to remove the worst of the ink, Lady would be sporting blue eye shadow for the foreseeable future.

Visions of a leisurely lunchtime—the ham-and-cheese sandwich stowed in the teachers' lounge's refrigerator, a walk with her coworkers—faded away. It was more important to handle this behavior issue. She turned back to the child. "Landon, sit down and tell me what you were doing."

"She needed decorating." He looked at his hands, also stained with blue. "Can I go to lunch?"

"Why on earth did you think she needed decorating? We don't do things like that to animals. The ink could hurt her."

He shrugged and stared at the floor.

So he wasn't going to explain. Probably, he couldn't. Being a new kid in a boarding school for boys with issues was reason enough to act out.

She looked around the library, trying to figure out an appropriate consequence that wasn't too harsh. She wasn't going to have him scrub Lady's face, but maybe he could clean up something else instead, she decided. And working together might give her a chance to know the new boy a little better, even help him feel he had a place here.

"I'm going to have to spend extra time cleaning the marker off Lady," she said, "so I'd like for you to help me straighten up the library before you go to lunch. You can start with picking up the paper on the floor." She pointed to the corner of the room, where several crumpled balls of paper had missed the trash can. "After that, you can help me put our chairs back at the tables."

"Fine." Landon blew out a heavy, dramatic sigh and headed toward the messy corner.

Relieved that he hadn't gotten belligerent, Emily reshelved the books she'd been showing the kids. The library was small, but the shelves lined with books gave her a peaceful, expansive feeling. You were never trapped when there was a book to read. She'd have to try to find out Landon's reading tastes.

Lady had been watching Emily, but now she rested her blue-tinted head on her paws. Obviously, the service dog hadn't detected any unusual nervousness or tension. And she was right. Kids misbehaving was just part of the job at Bright Tomorrows Academy.

The new handyman strode into the library and looked from Landon, crushing down paper into the overfull wastebasket, to Emily, and back again. Then he knelt in front of the boy. "Why are you cleaning? You're a student here."

Seeing the two dark heads together made it click for Emily: they had to be father and son. New handyman, new student. No wonder the handyman had paid extra attention to the class. His son was in it.

Landon ducked away from his dad and hustled over to the chairs, moving them back to their original locations at tables. He didn't volunteer why he was in trouble, of course.

Emily opened her mouth to explain and then snapped it closed again as the handyman advanced on her, brows drawn together, mouth pressed into a flat line. He gestured at Landon. "He's the custodian's kid, not the custodian," he growled in a low voice, obviously not wanting Landon to hear. "I won't have him doing cleaning work."

He was big and angry, and Emily sucked in a breath and took a step backward. Lady got to her feet, trotted toward them and pushed her nose into Emily's hand.

The movement caught the handyman's attention, and his eyes widened. "What happened to your dog?"

Emily was tempted to take another step back, away from his looming intensity, but she forced herself to stay put. "Landon happened," she explained. "He decided the dog needed to be more colorful. Since he made a mess, I asked him to clean up a mess as a consequence. I'm Emily Carver," she added, sticking out her hand.

"Dev McCarthy," he said, automatically shaking hers, still frowning.

His hands were callused, as you'd expect from his line of work. Muscular arms strained the sleeves of his polo shirt, and his hair was graying at the temples, though he didn't look much older than Emily was. Forty at most.

The lines in his forehead smoothed out, though a slight frown remained.

Having defused the situation and calmed everyone down, as usual, Lady nudged Emily one last time, glanced up at her and then settled on the floor a few feet away.

Landon finished straightening the chairs but didn't approach his father and Emily. He stood beside one of the tables, fidgeting from foot to foot.

Emily glanced from the child to Dev. "As far as I'm concerned, he's made up for what he did and can go to lunch," she said quietly. "I'll walk him down, unless you'd like to talk with him first?"

"I can walk my own kid to lunch." He beckoned to Landon, and the two of them left the library.

"Thanks for helping," Emily called after the boy.

He glanced back and then hurried after his father.

That went well. Not.

In her tiny office in the back of the library, Emily checked her phone. Three messages from the same number, and...uh-oh.

She sank into her desk chair and returned the call, identifying herself. "Is my mom okay?"

"She's fine." The business office manager's voice sounded impatient. "It's about your account."

Emily blew out a breath and leaned back, staring up at the industrial-tile ceiling. "I know my payment is late. I had an unexpected car repair, but my tax refund check will arrive any day, and as soon as it does, I'll send the money."

"With the late fee," the woman reminded her.

"Right. Of course." She ended the call, adding up numbers in her mind. She knew the amount of the late fee because she'd paid it before.

Which just spoke to the fact that her situation wasn't sustainable.

But Mom was getting great care—care that Emily couldn't provide at home. Her stomach churned.

"What's wrong?" Her friend Hayley, who managed food services at the school, stuck her head in the door. "You didn't come walk. We missed you."

"Little problem with the new student. And then a call from Mom's care center. I'm late paying."

"Ugh." Hayley came in and perched on the edge of Emily's desk. "Hey, did you meet the new handyman? He's good to look at."

"Nope. Not interested." No one who looked like the new handyman would give her a second glance.

Which was fine. She had plenty of problems without adding a handsome, surly man into the mix. Plus, she'd had her chance and she'd blown it, lost everything. She didn't deserve another try at relationships.

"You're not doing the whole 'I don't deserve happiness' thing, are you? Because you *do* deserve it. No matter what happened in the past, we're forgiven and can make a fresh start."

"Right." At least in theory, but the practical truth was that Emily would never let herself get involved with a man, given what had happened in the past, even though her biological clock seemed to tick louder every year. "I need to focus on making some extra money. Do you need any part-time help in the kitchen? I could work the dinner shift."

"You shouldn't work two jobs, should you? Think of the stress."

As if to prove Hayley right, Lady shoved her nose into Emily's hand, then leaned against her.

Emily stroked the big dog, and her nerves settled. "I'm pretty sure I'll have to find a second job," she said. "And if I do, I'd rather work with you, here at Bright Tomorrows, than flip burgers in town."

"And I'd love to have you work with me, but we're fully staffed. No budget for a new hire." Hayley's dark eyes were warm with sympathy. "God will help you find a way."

Emily sure hoped so. And the sooner, the better.

At the end of the school day, Dev waited for the students to be dismissed to their dorm parents. The few day students boarded their vans or climbed into cars. When it was Landon's turn for dismissal, the boy looked around for Dev, and there was relief in his eyes when he saw his father.

Which just about gutted Dev. Landon had lived mostly with his mom, back in Denver, and she hadn't always been reliable about things like picking up her son at the scheduled time. Especially as she'd gotten more into dating. When the marriage had ended three years ago, she hadn't wanted Dev to have but every other weekend with Landon. As time went on, she'd allowed more and more visitation until Dev had Landon most weekends. Just last month, he'd found the opening at Bright Tomorrows and proposed taking Landon full-time. Frustrated with Landon's school and behavior problems, she'd agreed with the plan, and here they were.

Dev had plenty of inadequacies, but he'd do

everything within his power to show up for his son, because he knew from personal experience what it was like to be the last kid left waiting in front of the school.

And he'd also do his best to be a good parent, which meant teaching interpersonal skills. He beckoned to Landon. "We need to apologize to Ms. Carver before we go home."

"Aw, I already did her chores," Landon protested. "And Lady—that's her dog—is okay. She said so."

"We didn't tell her we were sorry. Come on."

Landon fell into step beside him, dragging his feet. "You mean me."

"What?"

"Me. *I* need to tell her, not we."

At eight, Landon was starting to analyze the details of what Dev said, often with an eye toward rebelling against whatever Dev told him. "Truth is," Dev said, "I need to apologize as well. I was short with her when I saw you doing the cleaning."

"You're gonna apologize for that?"

"Uh-huh." Even though it might not be well received. Emily Carver, a reading teacher, of all things, had reason to be already set against Landon, although Dev hoped she wasn't that quick to judge a kid. And she might not think well of a lowly handyman like Dev.

But for his son's sake, to set a good example, he'd put in an effort.

There was another reason as well. Dev had gotten the impression, from report cards and from a few things his ex had said, that Landon was struggling in school. It didn't seem all that serious a problem, and Dev wasn't too worried about it, but he also didn't want Landon to face the challenges Dev faced himself. That was why he'd been watching Ms. Carver's class so closely. If Landon needed a tutor, Dev wanted to find him a good one. Ms. Carver seemed like she just might fit the bill, though after his annoyance with her earlier today, he felt less sure.

As they approached the library, Landon hung back and spoke to a kid passing by. That was good—Dev wanted his son to make friends in the new school, so he continued on to the library door and stood waiting.

He could see Ms. Carver in her glassed-in cube of an office, her dog beside her. Reddish-brown hair to her shoulders, in a simple style that suited her matter-of-fact attitude and friendly smile. She seemed to be on the phone— that or she was talking to herself. She looked young and fresh-faced, but he'd seen the tiny wrinkles fanning out from her eyes and figured she wasn't that much younger than he was. She just wore it better.

Beyond the office were the library's shelves and shelves of books. They held worlds that were closed to Dev, but with the help of this school, they'd be open to Landon. It was worth the pay cut to get the free tuition and pull Landon away from bad influences, including his mother's flavor-of-the-week boyfriends. Her unsteady lifestyle had meant lots of school moves for Landon, and the academic struggles that went along with that. Dev hoped a consistent stretch at a private school would solve those problems quickly. If not, he'd get serious about hiring a tutor, maybe even pretty-but-uptight Ms. Carver. So it was time to make nice.

He looked back to see his son wandering toward him, kicking the wall every few steps.

"Come on, Landon," he said. "Now."

Landon walked marginally faster, and they entered the library together.

He cleared his throat. "Ms. Carver?"

She looked up, but her phone buzzed. She raised a finger, her face apologetic. "Be right with you," she said and then took the call.

"Thank you for calling me back. I need something part-time. Right." She listened for a moment. "Right, I understand. Is it okay if I call you back in a couple of weeks and see if anything has opened up?" She listened another few seconds. "Sure. Thanks."

She came out the half-opened door and flipped back her hair, which he was already starting to recognize as a nervous gesture. "Hi, Landon. Mr. McCarthy."

"You can call me Dev."

"And I'm Emily," she said with an impersonal smile. "Reading teacher and librarian for Bright Tomorrows. It's a small school, so we tend to play more than one role here."

He'd already realized that, when he'd walked around with the school principal and seen that he was expected to fix the furnace and repair the malfunctioning bell system as well as cleaning classrooms and trimming hedges. Which was fine with him. He had a knack for fixing things, and he liked to work hard.

He refocused on Emily, who was looking at him expectantly. "We wanted to apologize," he said.

"No need. We're fine."

"No." His mouth was dry and he swallowed, conscious of the need to set an example, not just of the importance of apologies, but of how to do them. "I spoke sharply to you earlier, and I had no call to do that. I'm sorry."

Her face broke into a genuine, open smile that looked like sunshine. "Thank you. Really, it's fine."

It was hard to look away from her, but he

made himself turn toward his son, put a hand on the boy's shoulder. "Landon?"

Landon squared his shoulders. "I'm sorry I put marker on your dog. Is she okay?"

There was that sunshiny smile again. "Thank you for apologizing. Lady's fine." She turned and spoke to the dog, and the white poodle mix stood, stretched with her front legs out and back end high, and then trotted over.

The dog's eyes were now surrounded by pale blue circles. Apparently, Emily had gotten some of the marker out of the dog's fur, but not all. Definitely not a good start for Landon.

But Emily seemed to take it in stride. She slipped off the dog's red vest. "Would you like to pet her?" she asked Landon. "You can, as long as she's out of harness."

"Yeah!" Landon knelt in front of the dog and stuck out a tentative hand. As far as Dev knew, the boy hadn't had much experience with animals, but he seemed to love them.

Emily pulled a toy out of a basket just inside her office door. She knelt beside Landon. "You'd be doing me a favor if you'd play with her for a few minutes. She's been sitting still most of the day. It's not easy being a service dog."

Landon took the tug toy with a shy smile at Emily, and Dev was pretty sure the boy had just become a fan of the pretty librarian.

Dev was starting to like her better himself, because she wasn't holding Landon's earlier misbehavior against him. Instead, she seemed to be trying to build a bridge and help Landon feel comfortable at his new school. Dev appreciated that.

He wondered what kind of service dog Lady was, since Emily had no visible disability. But it would be rude to ask her outright.

Landon had no such scruples. As he played a game of tug-of-war with the dog, he looked up at Emily. "How come you have a service dog?"

Dev winced. "Landon. That's Ms. Carver's private business."

"It's okay. All the kids know." She glanced up at Dev and then knelt down to the level of Landon and the dog. "I had something bad happen to me, and I still get nervous and upset sometimes. Lady helps me stay calm."

"What was the—" Landon cut off his question and looked up at Dev. "Sorry. It's your private business."

Good. Dev gave Landon an approving smile and a slight head nod.

Dev was curious, too. Sounded like a PTSD dog, making him wonder if Emily was a veteran. It was hard to imagine the petite, almost delicate woman in a uniform, but that was just his own sexism talking. All kinds of women did all kinds of things in the military these days.

She straightened and brushed her hands together. "How are you both liking the school? Where'd you move from?"

"It's a good change for both of us, I think," Dev said, because Landon wasn't answering. "We moved from Denver."

"Great city. You'll find it a lot quieter here." She flipped her hair again, and a whiff of strawberry tickled his nose.

Longing flashed through him, hard and sharp. He missed being close with a woman, but that wasn't on his playlist, not now. He needed to focus on Landon.

"Quiet's good," he said, stepping back. "We don't want to keep you. I'm sure you're eager to get home at the end of a school day."

"I definitely get tired, but it's a good tired." She stepped back into her office and started loading books into an old-fashioned brown satchel. "We just got a pile of new books in, and I'm eager to dig in. Book nerd," she added.

A skittery feeling turned his stomach over. "Uh-huh. Landon, we need to go," he said.

Since his divorce, he'd stayed well away from women who might discover his reading problems. No way was he inviting the kind of disrespect and ridicule he'd gotten from his ex because he couldn't read well.

He needed to keep his distance from pretty, complicated Emily Carver. Even if he did ask her to tutor Landon, he'd make sure everything was strictly professional.

"Come on," he repeated to Landon, who was dawdling, playing with the dog.

Landon stood immediately, and Dev realized he'd spoken more sharply than he'd intended.

"I'll walk out with you," Emily said easily. She slipped Lady's service vest and harness back onto her, then picked up her loaded satchel, struggling a little.

Dev held out a hand. "I can carry that out for you."

She looked surprised. "Oh! Well, sure. Thanks."

It was as if she wasn't used to a man helping her out, making Dev wonder even more about her background. He picked up her satchel, and the three of them headed out of the school.

The silence between them felt awkward, at least to Dev, and he was relieved when they got to the parking area. He handed her the heavy satchel. "We'll be seeing you," he said, turning toward the road that led to the staff cabins.

"Actually, I live over in the cabins." She and her dog turned in the same direction.

"We live there, too." Landon sounded amazed. "We just moved in."

Her eyebrows lifted a fraction at the same moment that Dev got a sinking feeling. "Which one?" he asked.

"Cabin six," she said.

"We're in five." And a pretty reading teacher wasn't exactly whom he'd have chosen as a next-door neighbor.

Seeing her on a day-to-day basis, at home as well as at work, was just going to rub in the fact that he couldn't dream of connecting with a woman whose life was all about books and reading.

He had to keep his distance to conceal the embarrassing fact that he could barely read.

Chapter Two

The week flew by quickly, as most of them did at the busy school, and the weekend passed even faster. Emily spent most of Saturday with friends in town, not *necessarily* to avoid her new neighbors, but partly so. She felt a little too intrigued by Dev, and she wanted to avoid letting that interest build at all, since she'd never pursue it. And Landon…well. He was a cute kid, and he tugged at her heartstrings. That happened to all teachers, and wasn't necessarily a bad thing. But for Emily, with her anxiety issues, it felt wrong and dangerous to develop an affection for Landon.

Since the school started with grade three, this was the first year she'd taught kids the same age her son, James, would have been, if he'd lived. Landon had the same coloring, too, right down to the unusual hazel eyes, and for some reason, that combination was kicking her hard. Better to avoid the pair entirely.

Sunday, she drove an hour south to visit her mother, and Sunday evening, as the sun set over the Rockies, she pulled into her little driveway and shot up a prayer of thanks. Her loud, smoking beater of a car had made the weekly trip once more.

Across the road from the cabins, a lively picnic was in progress, with several people already sitting around a wooden table. At the sight, the tension left her shoulders.

She carried in her things, Lady trotting beside her. She really should go straight to bed. The drive and the visit had taken it out of her, and she had a busy week coming up. But after spending time with her mother and having an unpleasant conversation with the accounts manager of the Alpine Care Center, she needed cheering up.

"We'll go see our friends for just a little while but make it an early night," she said to Lady. *Do not pass go, do not look to the right or left, especially the left.*

Of course, she *did* look to the left, just in time to see Dev and Landon coming out the door of their cabin.

She considered turning around and going right back in. Although she and Dev had waved to each other last week, and although Landon had come to reading class all week, she hadn't had individual interactions with them.

Despite that, the handyman and his endearing son had been on her mind throughout the trip.

She'd be concerned about any new colleague or student. Wouldn't she?

"Hey, Emily."

Dev's low voice danced along her nerve endings, heating her face as she turned.

"Hi, Landon," she said, deliberately greeting the boy first. "Hi, Dev. Are you going to the picnic?"

"Didn't know about it, so probably not," Dev said. "It's a school night."

"That's the whole point of it." She leaned against the split-rail fence that stood between their yards. "Sunday nights can be gloomy. So the staff usually has a get-together to cheer up and stretch out the weekend as long as possible. You're welcome to come." She smiled at Landon. "It probably doesn't sound fun to hang around a bunch of teachers, but the boys usually have some kind of activity in the residence houses on Sunday nights. I'm sure you could join in."

"Actually," Dev said, "we came out because I heard your car."

Emily sighed. "I'm sorry. I know it's loud. You probably smelled it, too."

"Want me to take a look at it?"

She tipped her head to one side. "Really?"

"Dad's good at fixing cars," Landon said.

"I couldn't pay you—"

Something flashed in his eyes. "I'm just being neighborly. If you don't want me to look at it, it's okay."

"You can't afford to turn down an offer like that," Stan, the tall, white-haired math teacher, said as he approached from the cabin on the other side of Dev's. He stuck out a hand to Dev. "Stan Davidson. Seen you around the past week but didn't get the chance to say hello."

Dev greeted him and introduced Landon. It turned out Landon already knew the math teacher, and from the boy's frown, Emily guessed the connection wasn't a positive one.

"Wouldn't mind seeing what's going on under the hood of that vehicle myself," Stan said. "It'd probably be better if the whole thing just caught fire, so you could get the insurance money."

Emily flinched. *He means well, and he doesn't know what happened to you.* She thanked them both and left the two men, and Landon, studying her car.

As she approached the picnic, Hayley detached from the group. "You made it back! How was your visit?"

"It was good. Better than usual."

"Meaning..."

"Meaning Mom knew me." She wrinkled her nose. "But she didn't remember any of the bad stuff, which is a blessing. She was in a good mood."

"That's great. I'm so glad." Hayley put an arm around her. She was Emily's best friend, and one of the few people who knew about the family tragedy that had darkened Emily's past.

"They take such good care of her. And they're willing to work with me on payments, but the fact is, I need to pull together more money."

Beside her, Lady poked her nose into Emily's hand, reminding her to take deep breaths and relax her muscles.

Stan walked toward the picnic, Landon beside him. It looked like Stan was lecturing, and Landon grimaced and then took off running back toward his cabin.

"I hear he's not doing so well," Hayley said.

"Who, Landon? What do you mean?"

"Academics."

They both watched as Dev straightened from where he'd been looking under the hood of Emily's car and spoke sharply to Landon. Emily couldn't hear the words, but she could recognize a scolding, even from this distance.

"Poor kid," she murmured. "It can't be easy living next door to two of your teachers when you're eight years old."

Hayley frowned. "Eight. That's about how old your son would have been. Are you thinking about that?"

Emily bit her lip and nodded, glancing around to make sure nobody had heard Hayley's blunt words. Fortunately, the five or six other people in the gathering were clustered together, roasting hot dogs over a small fire someone had built, talking and laughing.

She looked at the fire and got stuck there, spiraling into the horror that had happened six years ago. Hearing her mother's screams, but not her husband's, nor her baby's, because it was too late. The sirens, the sooty firefighters, the mess of water.

They'd done their best, but it hadn't been enough.

Leaving her baby with her difficult husband so she could go out with friends had been stupid enough, but when Mom was in the mix... It had been a huge mistake, one she'd paid for all too dearly. Mom had paid, too, since she'd left a pan burning on the stove and caused the fire. She was devastated when she remembered what she'd done, which thankfully was less and less often.

But James, her sweet two-year-old baby boy, and her husband as well, had paid with their lives.

"Hey, c'mon, let's get a hot dog," Hayley said. "You probably didn't have much to eat today."

Emily stroked Lady beside her and fought her way back to the present moment. "No, I didn't. A hot dog sounds good." She forced the words through a tight throat, but she got them out. "But I don't think I can…" She gestured toward the fire, her throat closing again.

She was getting better, but she knew her limits. She couldn't roast a hot dog over a fire without losing it.

"I'll make you one in a minute," Hayley said. "We've got company." She glanced past Emily.

Emily looked over her shoulder and saw Dev heading toward them, a concerned frown on his face, wiping oily hands on a rag. "I fixed the split hose that's causing your car to smoke like that," he said, "but it's temporary. The car needs a major overhaul."

It wasn't news to her, but hearing it said aloud pushed a heavy weight onto her shoulders. "Thank you for fixing what you could," she said, her throat still feeling tight. "You didn't have to do that. I appreciate it."

Hayley stood close beside her, and Lady leaned against her other side. Emily was enveloped by love, and she was truly grateful.

She just didn't know how to solve her money problems, which seemed to loom bigger all the time.

"Look," Hayley said, "you can do the car fix with a credit card, if need be."

"I don't like doing that." Her husband had gotten them into debt, and she'd had a terrible time paying it off. "Will the car run for a while?" she asked Dev. "I have to make weekly trips to Fort Collins, about an hour away. Aside from that and a stop at the grocery, that's all I need to drive."

He frowned. "Baby it along, and make sure you're not driving at night or on lonely stretches of highway."

"Hard to avoid in Colorado." She straightened. "But it's not your problem. I appreciate what you did, so much."

She'd just redouble her search for a second job. The stress of working two jobs might affect her, but it couldn't be worse than this money stress.

And besides, working a second job would keep her from being around her new neighbors.

The dad, with the piercing, soulful eyes and the talent for car repair.

And the son, who made her think of all she'd lost.

After cleaning up from the car repair, Dev reluctantly agreed to go out to the picnic with Landon.

As they approached, his eyes went immediately to Emily. Probably because she was at the center of the group. She'd seemed blue before, but now she was laughing at something the white-haired math teacher had said. The math teacher who'd apparently been scolding Landon for not turning in his math homework last week.

The sense that they were a community and he was on the outside was familiar. And a bunch of teachers was just the group to heighten his feelings of inadequacy. But for Landon's sake, he'd go make nice. Set the example of being friendly, not having a chip on his shoulder, not taking things personally.

And if Stan the math teacher gave Landon a hard time again, Dev would take the man aside and have a word with him.

"Hey, it's our new superhero!" That was Annabel Andrews, the art teacher. "This guy made the furnace stop blowing nonstop heat into the art studio. I can finally teach without the windows open."

"And he *got* the cafeteria windows open, so we're not eating surrounded by the smell of kid sweat," Hayley said, then glanced at Landon. "Sorry, kiddo. I'm not talking about you, but when you get a group of teen and preteen boys in a small room and turn up the heat, things get smelly."

"I know, I've smelled a locker room," Landon said wryly, and everyone laughed. It made Dev proud of his son, that he could speak to a group of adults without acting all shy and embarrassed.

"He's not going to live with the boys?" Stan asked, his voice hearty.

"No. He needs to stay with me." No way was he gaining custody of his son and then shipping him off to boarding school, even if Landon's quarters would be just on the other side of the school grounds.

"The kids are seeing a movie tonight," Annabel said. "Something horrible, with monsters. I'm sure you could join them just for the movie, Landon, if you want to."

"Can I, Dad?"

It was a good plan. Landon would get to know some of the other boys better, and this group of teachers wouldn't have a student in their midst, inhibiting their conversation. "Sure, I'll walk you down. Where is it?" he asked the group.

"Big brick building behind the barn. Emily, could you show them?" That was Richard Cunningham, the vice principal of the school. Landon had already found out he was the man in charge of discipline.

"Um…sure. Of course." She forced a smile. "If we hurry, we'll get there in time for you to see the beginning of the movie, I think. They usually start at eight."

She led the way to the road and then stepped back to walk beside them. The sun's glow was fading behind the mountains, but it still cast enough light to see the rocks, tall pines and thin, lacy leaves of the wildflowers that would burst into bloom next month.

"It's cold out here," Landon said. He was walking close to Dev, Emily on the other side.

Dev found the air bracing, and the stars, beginning to grow visible, seemed thicker, denser than back in the city. It reminded him of living with his favorite foster family, the ones with the farm. He'd lived there for three years and had learned his basic handyman skills there.

The placement had been great, until it ended. Every placement had ended for Dev, some quicker than others. He hadn't been a bad kid—

no worse than most, anyway—but his school struggles had made him act out.

Kind of like Landon. But that was going to change.

Landon and Emily were chatting about something, and Dev was glad. Emily was a good influence on his son, Dev could already tell. She didn't come on too strong, but she was truly interested in kids and seemed to respect what they had to say. Even now, she was listening closely as Landon went on and on about a movie he'd seen. She actually asked relevant questions about the plot and actors and said she wanted to see it, too.

More than Dev had done the last three times Landon had given him a blow-by-blow account of that same movie, he had to admit.

"Here we are," Emily said. She slid open a barn-style door and spoke to the woman inside. The smell of pizza filled the air.

"Movie's just starting," the woman said after introducing herself to Dev and greeting Landon. "Get yourself a drink and some pizza and find a seat."

Landon grabbed three slices, the hot dog he'd just eaten notwithstanding. He made his way to an empty seat, already stuffing pizza into his mouth.

"He's going to fit in fine," Emily said as they

headed back toward the bonfire. "He seems like a good kid, comfortable in his own skin."

"He is." That was the wonder of Landon: even with divorced parents, a dad with reading issues that had held him back professionally and a mom who was none too dependable, he was essentially secure. "I mean, I guess none of the kids here are what would really be considered good kids, since they're at a school for conduct issues."

She shrugged. "A lot of them made one mistake. Or they had school issues, undiagnosed learning disabilities and the like, and they acted out."

He liked that she saw it that way, realized that some things weren't a kid's fault. "You don't have kids?"

She didn't answer, didn't seem to hear. Instead, she knelt and focused on something on Lady's paw.

Dev breathed in the sharp, pine-scented air and lifted his face to study the emerging stars. So many, so far away.

"The stars are pretty, aren't they?" She stood and lifted her face to them, and they started to stroll again. He was conscious that she hadn't answered his question about kids, but maybe it had been a rude one. Women were always getting asked intrusive questions about their reproductive plans and issues—at least, that was what his ex had said.

"Do they make you feel small, the stars?" she asked him.

He'd never thought about it. "I guess…they make me feel like there are infinite possibilities." His cheeks heated. He wasn't normally the poetic type.

"I like that," she said. "Infinite possibilities. Hmm. What would you wish for?"

He knew the answer before she'd even gotten the question out, but no way was he sharing it with her. So he said another wish, just as important if not more. "I want Landon to have everything he wants."

"So you're planning to spoil him?"

The question made his head whip around to glare at her, and then he realized she was joking. "Yeah, I'm buying him a pony and a sports car," he joked back.

"Get me a sports car, too, while you're at it."

He laughed. "What color?"

"Is there any color other than red?"

He could picture her in a sports car, her hair flying in the wind. "You'd look good in a red convertible."

She snorted. "Right. But back to Landon. Does he actually have a conduct issue, or did you just enroll him here because you got the job?" As soon as the words were out, she lifted her hands. "Sorry. That's personal and I have no right to know it, not unless it affects his work in my class."

"It's okay. He's like what you said before. He made one mistake." Then he wondered whether he was making excuses for Landon, like Roxy always did. He didn't want Landon to catch that habit, so he corrected himself. "It was a serious mistake, and the fact that there were serious consequences is good for him. He needs to learn to take responsibility for mistakes he makes."

"What did he do?" she asked, her voice curious, and then she clapped her hand over her mouth. "There I go again. Sorry."

"It's okay," he said. He figured she'd find out soon enough. He'd worked in a school before and knew that gossip spread faster than the flu. "He set a fire."

Chapter Three

The next day Emily was still reeling from the revelation that Landon had set a fire. So it just figured that she'd look at her individual consultation schedule and see Landon's name on it, in the last slot of the day. *Diagnostic Reading Test* was the notation beside his name.

She focused on reshelving books while she waited for him to arrive. It was no more than she deserved. If working with a child exactly the same age, coloring and gender her own son would have been—a kid who'd set a *fire* of all things—was part of the job, well, she'd suck it up and do it well. She owed Landon the help and support.

Her thoughts flickered to Landon's father. He'd noticed her gasp about the fire, of course, and had quickly explained that no one had been hurt. Landon had set the fire in a trash can in the school restroom after something upsetting had happened in class—Dev wasn't sure what—and he'd actually been trying to put it out when the fire alarm had gone off. But the school had a zero-tolerance policy for dangerous actions on the part of students, and now, he was barred from any regular schools in his own district. It had seemed like a good time for a change.

She'd been curious about Landon's mother, how she fit in, but Dev hadn't said anything about that. He'd only said that he'd gotten custody and permission to move Landon to Bright Tomorrows, two hours northwest of Denver.

She went back into her office and checked on Lady, who was napping on her rug. And then Lady lifted her head, and stood, and Landon was at the door.

"I hafta work with you," he said. He came into the library and dumped the contents of his backpack on the table, shoulders slumped. The cheerful kid from last night was gone.

She smiled at him. "You *get* to work with me, at least for today," she said. "But first, Lady wants to say hello. She perked right up when you came in." She slid the dog's harness off and let her go to Landon. Though she was Emily's service dog, she was good for the students, too. In practice, she was an unofficial therapy dog for the school. Not exactly best practice, according to the service dog training facility where Emily had gotten her and learned to work with her. But given Emily's life and her job, and Lady's personality, it all made sense.

Sure enough, Landon's tension eased.

"Okay, let's look at some books," she said, conscious that she only had half an hour with Landon.

He frowned. "Can Lady come?"

Normally, she wouldn't have done it, thinking the dog would be a distraction, but it was the last class of the day. Plus, she'd developed feelings for Landon. Which probably wasn't healthy, but there it was. "Sure, she can come. She might want us to look at the dog books first."

"She doesn't read books," Landon scoffed, but when she led him and Lady to the section where the animal books were shelved, he seemed marginally interested. They both knelt down to look at the low shelf.

"Go ahead and pull out three or four books that look good to you," she said. "Then we'll take a look and see which ones would be right for you to read." She always found that having students choose their own reading material worked best.

Landon pulled out a big encyclopedia of dogs and then a couple of books about specific breeds. Then he grabbed another featuring assistance animals, and one more about K-9 police dogs.

"Good choices," she said. "Now, let's do the finger test to see which is the best for you to read."

His mouth twisted to one side.

"You've probably done it before. Hold up one finger for each word you don't know on the first page."

He grabbed the encyclopedia of dogs, opened it up and looked at the first page. "I can read all the words," he said within seconds.

She was pretty sure he hadn't even glanced at the text but rather was drawn to the color photos of dogs. "You need to read it aloud," she said gently.

He looked at the text page for a minute and then thrust it aside. "I don't like this book."

"It's pretty hard," she said. "Want to try another?"

He picked up the one about K-9 police dogs. Good. It was at a second-grade reading level at most.

Landon opened to the first page, looked it over. Then, suddenly, he stood and hurled the book across the room. "I don't wanna read now! Reading is dumb!" He kicked at the other books.

"Landon! Stop it." She pulled the scattered volumes out of the way of his kicking feet. "We treat books with respect. Especially library books. They're for everyone."

"Not for me!" He rubbed a fist under his eye and ran toward the door.

His father was coming in, and Landon crashed into him. Dev caught the boy by the upper arms. "Hey, hey, no running in school. What's going on?"

Emily took a moment to shelve the books, all but the one he'd thrown. Dev had led Landon back into the library.

"She said books are for everybody, but they're not for me." Landon kicked at a table leg.

"What's this all about?" Dev asked Emily.

"I did say books are for everyone," she said, deliberately calming her voice. "We were talking about taking good care of books, after Landon threw one and kicked some others."

"Whoa. You can't do that." Dev's voice went deeper, and Landon looked just a little scared.

She picked up the police dog book and held it out to Dev. "This is the one he threw," she said. "I think he was frustrated because it looks so interesting, but it's a little too hard for him to read."

A pained look crossed Dev's face, so quickly she might have imagined it. "You need to apologize," he told Landon. "And if Ms. Carver wants to assign you another chore, you need to do it. You'll definitely have an extra chore at home."

"If you're giving him a consequence, that's plenty," Emily said. "And maybe you two would like to check out the book. Landon, after you've done your chore, your dad can read it with you."

Identical frowns crossed the two faces.

"He won't read it to me," Landon said.

So much for her brilliant idea.

"That's not my job, it's yours." Dev's voice was sharp as he handed the book back to her.

"Fine." Emily pressed her lips together to keep from snapping at them both. She carried the book back to the shelf to give herself time to cool down.

Why did men think they didn't need to model reading, or that the job of reading aloud fell to the mother? She took a couple of deep breaths. Lady, who'd been dozing in her office, came trotting out to her side.

She walked back toward Dev and Landon. Dev stood, arms crossed, while Landon loaded schoolbooks and papers back into his backpack. Clearly Landon had been scolded; he was blinking away tears.

"Tell her you're sorry."

"I'm sorry."

"Tell her what you're sorry for."

"I'm sorry I threw and kicked the books."

"Apology accepted." She felt the strongest urge to reach out and give Landon a hug. He was still just a little boy, really. "We can meet another day to talk about reading."

He nodded, looking down at the floor.

She looked up at Dev. "And maybe you and I should have a talk soon, too," she said.

He rubbed the back of his neck. "Sure," he said. "Sometime." And then he and Landon hurried out of the library.

Don't get involved. They're not your responsibility outside school hours.

Yet she had to admit, she was curious about the father-son pair. Drawn to them, even. Rudeness and all.

Friendliness and surliness alternated in both of them like a spinning coin—you never knew ahead of time which side would turn up. That wasn't unusual for new students here, and the reasons for it weren't her business. A better teacher would stay objective, focused on academics, and let the school counselors handle the emotions.

But there was something about the pair that kept plucking at her, drawing her in, making her care.

All the more reason to keep them at a distance, so she didn't start hoping for things she didn't deserve and couldn't have.

* * *

The day after Landon's disastrous reading experience, Dev walked into the school office and found a note in his little mailbox, one of a row in a wooden grid of open-front boxes. He studied the handwriting, then looked through the office's glass wall. Outside it, kids milled around in the lobby area, talking, laughing, play-punching each other.

He studied the note again, the letters swimming before his eyes, then glanced over at Mrs. Henry, the office secretary. "Forgot my glasses," he said, holding the note far away from him and squinting at it. "What's this about?"

"Let me see."

He handed her the note, relieved.

She looked at it and laughed. "Dr. Green has terrible handwriting. She wants to see you in her office sometime this morning, at your convenience."

"Thanks." He smiled at her. "No time like the present, I guess."

He tapped on the principal's half-opened door. "Dr. Green? You wanted to see me?"

"Come in," she said from behind her computer, and he walked into a book-lined office furnished with an old, scarred desk and gray metal filing cabinets.

Ashley Green had hired Dev and was well

respected by students and staff alike, as far as Dev could see. Pretty, too, if you liked the buttoned-up type.

She peered out at him from behind thick glasses, then stood. "Ah, yes, Dev. And please, call me Ashley."

"Sure." Though she seemed like a formal-titles type. Every inch a principal and a boss.

"Thank you for stopping in. I need to talk to you about Landon. Close the door, would you? And then have a seat."

Dev's stomach turned over as he closed the door, then sat in one of the chairs in front of her desk. She picked up a paper file and then sat in the chair beside him.

"Is Landon in trouble?" he asked. He'd punished the boy for throwing the book, but he hadn't explored the incident in too much detail. It struck too close to home.

Had Emily ratted Landon out?

But he shouldn't think of it that way. It might be that she was obligated to report the incident.

"No, he's not in trouble," she said. "He's a nice boy and seems to be fitting in well."

"Okay, good." Then what was this about?

"But he's behind in academics." Ashley tapped the folder she held. "We always consult about new students after their first week, see whether their placement is correct and whether they need extra help. Landon's records indicate that he passed second grade last year, so he was placed in third grade. But he's not doing so well there, at least from the looks of things."

"He's still adjusting," Dev said. His head spun with worries. He'd never been in an academic conference about Landon before; Landon's mom had always handled that end of things, or at least she'd told him she was handling it. Only lately had he learned that Roxy had been a no-show at most of the conferences the teachers at Landon's old school had tried to schedule.

He didn't know whether he was even allowed to argue, if disagreeing with a principal was inappropriate, but what else could he do? "He's a very smart boy. It's just that everything's new to him."

"Of course," the principal said, her voice soothing. "It'll take him a while to get his feet on the ground, and maybe that's all this is. But all three of his teachers indicated that he didn't seem to pay attention to what they were writing on the board, though he did fine in class discussions. That's why we decided to have him visit Emily, but she said the preliminary reading test didn't go well. Didn't even happen, as a matter of fact."

"Right." He sighed. "I'm sorry Landon didn't behave. He was punished."

"Well, but more than that, we're wondering if he acted out because he's having problems with reading. It's at this grade level that those kinds of issues really catch up with kids, because they need to be able to read in various subjects, not just language arts."

"But he's so young," Dev said. "You can't expect him to read history or philosophy."

She smiled. "Of course not. But all children's textbooks require some reading skills. Science, social studies. Even math has word problems."

"Can't the teachers work with him?" He wondered whether Landon would get poorer treatment because he wasn't a tuition-paying student.

"Of course. Emily, in particular, can help him with reading skills."

"Good." His face heated as he remembered how he'd rudely told her that teaching Landon was her job. She'd only been making a normal suggestion, that he read to his son at home.

He thought of how she'd looked, shelving the books. Nimble, quick, athletic. She seemed to be in great shape, somehow not what he'd expect from a librarian and reading teacher.

She appealed to him like honey to a bear who'd just come out of hibernation. And he shouldn't feel that way, because a woman like her wouldn't have anything to do with a man like him, especially if she found out his secret inadequacy.

A better person would just breezily confess he had trouble reading, act confident, get help. But Dev wasn't that kind of person. Too many years of being told he was stupid and worthless. Words said when you were a kid really stuck with you, made you who you were. That was why he was always careful to boost Landon's self-image when he could.

But parents weren't the only influence. At Landon's age, peers and teachers played an increasingly big role in what he thought of himself.

He had to make sure Landon wasn't seen as stupid or treated as deficient.

"...I'd also like for you to think about the possibility of holding him back a grade," the principal was saying.

Dev tuned back in and stared at her. "What?"

"Having him repeat third grade might be the best thing to do. That way, he'd—"

"No." He barked out the word without thought, because he instantly knew holding Landon back would be the wrong thing to do.

She tilted her head to one side. "Of course it's early times, and we'll have to see how he does between now and the end of school. But if he can't catch up, if he fails in the final grading period, we really wouldn't have a choice."

"No way. I don't want him to repeat third grade." Dev gripped the arms of the chair, hard.

"We don't do social passes here at Bright Tomorrows." Her voice was firm. "And there's no shame in repeating a grade."

Yes, there is. Landon was already big for his age, and if he was held back a year, he'd be a giant. He'd be that big kid in the class who was behind the younger, smaller, smarter kids. Who was ridiculed and labeled.

Like Dev had been.

"You'll need to work with him, then," she said. "Sit with him while he's doing his homework. Help him understand his textbooks. Possibly, get him some extra tutoring, beyond what we do here at the school."

He nodded quickly, stood. "I'll do it. We'll get him caught up. Thanks, Ashley." He turned and hurried out of the office, even though he could tell from her face that she wasn't finished talking to him.

He walked down the hall, but the place seemed too stifling for him. Memories of his own childhood, going from new school to new school, having a week or so of grace until someone discovered his lack of academic skills—all of it pressed in on him.

He'd survived, but it had been miserable. He wanted so much more for Landon.

He strode out through the double doors and walked toward the river that wound its way beside the school. The water sparkled and rushed. It was a perfect stream for trout.

He wanted to take Landon fishing, teach him how to read the water, show him how to dig for bait. He wanted to fry up fish for dinner, fish they'd just caught that day. It was part of what he'd dreamed of when he'd gotten the chance to move to the mountains.

But it looked like Landon would have another use for his free time. Homework. Studying. Tutoring.

Landon needed help with homework. He needed someone to read him books that interested him. Someone to help him catch up and get on track to a better life.

But that person definitely wasn't Dev. Not when he could barely read himself.

He was going to have to suck it up and ask Emily to tutor Landon, even though the very notion made him a little sick, thinking how hard it would be to hide his own inadequacies from someone who was around all the time, tutoring his son.

He hated to admit to himself that the notion of spending more time around Emily revved him up, like an old, decrepit car engine finally turning over and starting to run. Which was ridiculous and wrong. He should advertise for another tutor, since Emily, off-limits Emily, awakened so much that had been safely dormant in him.

But he couldn't tame the excitement that stirred in him at the thought of working with her to help Landon. She was sweet and caring, the opposite of Landon's mom in many ways. She'd be good for Landon, he knew it.

He listened to the sound of the rushing water, smelled the sage-scented breeze and let it cool him. If Dev took Landon fishing, and he liked it, no doubt Emily would find him a book on fishing to read. She seemed to pay close attention to kids' interests and build on them.

The trouble was, if Landon brought home books and wanted help reading them, Dev couldn't help. And that awareness opened a hollow wound in his chest that no excitement about a pretty reading teacher could fill.

Chapter Four

It was the Saturday before Easter, and Emily was still feeling troubled about Dev and Landon and all they'd stirred up inside her. She hoped helping with the church's annual Easter Egg hunt would heal that, would help her get it off her mind and move her toward a sense of Easter peace.

Hayley, though, apparently had other ideas.

"I'm so glad you came early to help hide the eggs," she said, tucking a pink plastic one behind a rock. "I wanted to ask you how your reading lesson with Landon went, but with being away visiting my family, I haven't seen you."

"It went okay. Do you think we should put some of these out in plain sight, for the little kids?"

"Definitely. And some well hidden, because

they're letting kids up to age twelve participate. What do you mean, it went okay?"

Emily shrugged, placing a couple of eggs out in the open and then standing, pushing her hands on her lower back to stretch.

The white church nestled against the foothills that surrounded the town of Little Mesa. A couple of backpackers walked by, talking and laughing, no doubt headed for the popular hiking trail that skirted the town.

They were accompanied by a golden retriever with a small pack of his own. Beside Emily, Lady watched the other dog but didn't bark or lunge. "Good girl," Emily murmured and gave her a small treat.

She breathed in the pine-scented air from the foothills. *Calm. Peace.*

Hayley nudged her. "Come on, let's hide some in back. Was the session with Landon really that bad?"

So much for peace, but maybe it would help to talk to Hayley about it. "Cone of silence," she said, and Hayley nodded. "He got very upset when I tried to get him to read aloud. Threw a book, in fact. When his dad came to get him and I suggested they check out a book and read together, Dev told me helping Landon was my job."

Hayley frowned. "That doesn't sound like

Dev. From what I've seen, he seems like an involved dad."

"He does," Emily agreed, kneeling to tuck a couple of eggs in the stone wall that separated the church from the mountain. "Maybe he just doesn't think reading is important. Or maybe it doesn't seem manly to him. Lots of men are like that."

"Finished, ladies?" Nate Fisher came out the back door of the church and surveyed their work. "The kids are starting to arrive out front. I think Mrs. Poole has bunny ears for you."

Hayley raised an eyebrow. "Where are *your* bunny ears, Pastor?"

He grinned. "I have to put on the whole bunny suit. You got off easy with just the ears."

They went around front, and sure enough, Mrs. Poole, who ran most things in the church, handed them ears and directed them to their stations. Kids of all ages and sizes were trickling toward the church, and the sight stirred something deep inside Emily.

She was thirty-five, and she wasn't going to have the chance to have another baby, but that didn't mean she didn't care. In fact, her biological clock seemed to be functioning particularly well these days.

Maybe helping out at kids' events wasn't the

best way to gain a sense of peace and acceptance about her life.

"Senorita Emily!" A dark-haired little boy hurled himself into her arms. "I'm going to get all the eggs!"

She knelt to hug him. "There's a limit. Five eggs per kid, I think."

He pouted.

His grandmother appeared behind him and greeted Emily in Spanish, and they discussed the event and their Easter plans. "There's a short lesson for the children before the egg hunt starts," Emily explained. *"Muy corto,"* she added as Mateo's eyebrows drew together, holding her forefinger and thumb an inch apart. "And afterward, you'll get to run around and find all kinds of sweets, if it's okay with your *abuela*."

"I want the sweets first," he said, earning a short lecture from his grandmother.

Hayley came over and heard the tail end of the conversation. "Can you help? Unbeknownst to me, Pastor Nate scheduled me to teach the lesson, and I need someone to translate into Spanish." Some of the families in their church spoke Spanish as their primary language. One service each week was conducted in Spanish, but since church events brought all members together, Pastor Nate tried to make them bilingual. Emily was fluent in Spanish, while Hayley was a beginner.

Hayley taught a simple lesson about Christ's sacrifice and how sins could be forgiven because of it, and Emily translated, and the kids were adorable. "If I yelled at my brother, could I be forgiven?" one little girl asked, glancing at the toddler on her mother's lap.

"Yes, absolutely," Hayley said. "But we try to do better all the time, because we love Jesus."

"Will I be forgiven if I take some extra eggs?" Mateo asked with a grin, earning another frown from his *abuela*.

"Forgiven, yes, but there are likely to be consequences," Emily said.

She felt a longing for the simple faith the children had. A longing to ask if she, too, could be forgiven for her own sins, so much vaster than these children's.

Of course, she knew in her head that God was all powerful and could forgive all sins. But in her heart, she didn't quite believe it.

Once the egg hunt started, Emily and Hayley and the other helpers stayed busy. The little kids were allowed to go first, and when the bigger ones joined, they were warned to be careful of the smaller ones. Most of the kids were great about it, the older ones helping and sharing, and Emily was touched. Her skills at speaking Spanish came in handy a couple more times, and she reminded herself that life could be good as a single person, that she could do a lot of good.

She was starting to feel the peace she'd been looking for. To open to the reality of Easter, the reawakening of the spring world around her, the possibility of new life.

As she leaned against the stone wall, watching the colorfully dressed children running around to try to find the last eggs, she noticed someone running toward the church. Two people, actually.

Dev and Landon.

Landon's brow was wrinkled, and he kept turning to gesture toward Dev, beckoning for him to hurry up. He must realize he'd missed most of the egg hunt. Dev was yelling at him to slow down and watch for cars.

Both of them spotted Emily and came toward her.

Even though they'd parted on a bad note, a rude note.

Great. What was Dev going to do now— tell her it was her job to fix the egg hunt for Landon?

Dev slowed to a walk as Landon sprinted toward Emily.

She stood beside a shorter, older woman

as the activity of the egg hunt swirled around them. Wound down, unfortunately. It looked like things were over.

Emily looked fresh-faced and young in a pink sweater, jeans and bunny ears. He found himself wondering if she smelled like strawberries, the way she had last week.

As Landon approached and started talking to her, she held up a finger, indicating that he should wait until she'd finished her conversation with the older lady. Good. Dev caught up in time to catch the tail end of it; she was telling the woman, in Spanish, that it was fine that her grandson had snagged an extra egg, but maybe they could ask him to share it with someone who hadn't gotten their share.

"What's she saying, Dad?" Landon asked.

Dev explained. "It sounds like the hunt is over, but there may be a few kids with extra eggs who can share."

Emily glanced at him, looking surprised. *"Hablas español?"*

"Si, un poco." He normally didn't think much about the fact that he spoke and understood Spanish pretty well, but now he was glad. He smiled at the older lady. *"Buenas días, Señora,"* he added, and Emily introduced them. They chatted for a moment, and then the woman

excused herself and hurried over to a little boy who was stuffing candy into his mouth.

Landon was near tears. "I made us late and now I missed the hunt," he said, his voice shaky. He started to pet Lady, but Emily pointed to the service dog's vest and shook her head.

Landon's tears overflowed.

Dev tensed and then reminded himself to take deep breaths. Of course, it was okay for boys to cry, but that didn't mean it was comfortable for Dev to see it happen. He'd had one foster father who'd beaten him for it, and others who'd made fun, and he'd quickly learned not to show the softer emotions himself.

But he wanted Landon to have a different sort of childhood, different values. "There'll be other candy for Easter," he said, putting a hand on his son's shoulder.

"But I wanted to *hunt*!"

Emily snapped her fingers. "You know what? We may need someone to help us as things wind down. We kept count of all the eggs so nothing gets left around for animals to get into." She called to Hayley, the cafeteria head from the school, who also sported bunny ears. "Any eggs still missing?"

"Three," Hayley called back.

"I have a helper who will find them, maybe." She raised an eyebrow at Dev, who nodded permission, and she put an arm around Landon and guided him around the side of the church.

"Nice girl," said a voice behind Dev, and he turned to see his cousin Nate, who'd helped him get the job at Bright Tomorrows. "How's it going?"

"Everything's good now," Dev said. "You know Emily?" He didn't want to ask, but he couldn't help it; the woman made him curious.

"Yes. She hasn't had an easy time of it. Well, neither have you and I, for that matter, but her situation was a lot worse than ours."

"Really? She seems to have it together." Although she did have her service dog at her side today, like usual.

"She's resilient. But I pray for her."

Devon looked sharply at his cousin. "Why? Are you interested in her?"

Nate laughed. "No. I pray for a lot of people. You included." He lifted an eyebrow. "Sounds like *you're* interested."

Dev's face heated. "No. No way. A teacher's not my type."

"Dad! Dad!" Landon came running from behind the church, three eggs in his hands. Emily followed, laughing, a lilting sound like bells. The wind blew her hair across her face, and she brushed it back.

"You sure she's not your type?" Nate said in a low voice.

"Can it." He bent to look at Landon's eggs, then straightened and met Emily's eyes. "Thank you for helping him. I appreciate the second chance."

"Everyone needs a second chance sometimes," she said evenly, meeting his gaze.

Their eyes held for a moment longer than they should have.

Landon sat down on the ground and opened the first egg. Several pieces of brightly wrapped candy were there, along with a slip of pink paper. Landon studied it, then handed it up to Dev. "What's this say, Dad?"

Dev's insides constricted. Emily was standing there, and so was his cousin. He studied the paper, the letters dancing in front of him.

He was forty years old and couldn't read a piece of paper meant for kids. What did that say about him?

Given time, he might be able to puzzle it out. But not when he was on the spot, with an audience.

His heart rate picked up, heating his face, his whole body. Wasn't that just like a teacher, a pastor, a church, putting something to read inside an Easter egg? Ridiculous.

But she and Nate had been nothing but kind to him and Landon. It was wrong of him to be angry. He shouldn't—couldn't—let them see how he felt.

Mostly, he was mad at himself for being such an idiot.

He looked at the families around him and saw mothers and fathers oohing and aahing over their children's treasures. No doubt they were all easily able to read the papers to their children.

"Can I see?" Nate asked, taking the paper from Dev's hand. "I didn't get a chance to look these over before Mrs. Poole organized everyone and got the eggs stuffed." He read aloud. "'He is risen! He is not here.' Oh, good, the verses are in Spanish and English." He knelt and held the paper out to Landon. "See? There's a picture of an empty tomb. We'll talk about it more in church tomorrow."

"Cool." Landon was more occupied with the candy.

As for Dev, the sweat dripped down his back as his heart rate settled back to normal. Relief. Emily hadn't noticed anything.

Nate, though, was looking at him thoughtfully. His cousin the pastor was pretty smart. If he put what had just happened together with the kind of support he'd had to give Dev to help him get the job...yeah.

If he hadn't already, he might very soon guess Dev's secret.

The next day was Easter. After the sunrise service, Emily helped put chairs away. So did Landon and Dev. She hadn't realized that they were related to the pastor until yesterday, but now she could see a slight family resemblance. Both tall, square jawed, muscular. Landon, at eight, was headed in the same direction, big and strong for his age.

They walked out together to the parking lot. Emily was relieved they'd gotten friendly again, although she was also still irritated that he didn't want to help his son with reading. She wished them a happy Easter and got in her car.

When she turned it on—or tried to—nothing happened.

"Come on, come on..." She didn't need this delay. She needed to get going if she was going to make it over the mountain and to her mother's care center in time for the big Easter dinner.

She tried again, and this time the car turned over, made a horrible sound and died.

She let her head rest on the steering wheel for just a minute.

It was Easter. She *had* to visit her mom.

Granted, Mom might not even recognize her, know she was there or remember it later, but what if she did? What if today was a rare good day, and Emily missed it...and worse, Mom felt alone and abandoned on this holiday?

There was a knock on her car window. She turned her head to the side and recognized Landon's concerned face. She read his lips as he asked, "What's wrong, Miz Carver?"

She sighed and got out of the car. "It won't start," she said. She shivered in the cool mountain air. She'd worn an Easter dress, but it really wasn't warm enough for it. She'd welcomed the outdoor heaters Pastor Nate had put around the courtyard where they'd held the service.

Landon nodded. "That's what Dad thought. You can get a ride home with us."

"I was supposed to visit my mother," she said, biting her lip. She looked across the parking lot and saw Dev climbing out of his truck.

"My dad doesn't have time to fix your car today," Landon said as Dev approached, "because *my* mom's coming to see me today." He sounded excited.

Surprised, she looked at Dev.

"He's right, we do have to get back to the cabin," Dev said. "But we can run you home. At least you won't be stuck here."

"Come on, Ms. Carver, hurry!"

What else could she do? It wasn't as if she was going to fix the car herself, here in the church parking lot in her Easter finery.

Besides, she admitted to herself, she was curious about Landon's mother. What kind of woman had Dev chosen for a wife?

What kind of woman would let Dev and Landon go?

The ride back to the cabins went quickly. Landon chattered away about what he and his mother were going to do and what she might bring him.

Emily was grateful for the distraction. She felt awful about not seeing her own mom.

When they arrived at the cabins, a white SUV was pulling into Dev's driveway. Landon barreled out the moment the truck stopped. He ran toward the car. "Mom!"

Emily was watching him, so she saw the moment when he slowed, stopped and stepped back.

A woman got out of the passenger side. A man got out of the driver's side.

Dev muttered something under his breath, got out of the car and strode over.

There was nothing for Emily to do but get out, too. So she heard the unhappy little family drama.

"She brought her boyfriend," Landon said to his father, sounding deflated.

"He has a name," the woman said with a forced-sounding laugh. "Landon, Dev, this is Adam."

The man, a very handsome, fine-featured man in hiking clothes, stuck out a hand. "Glad to meet you both," he said.

Landon ignored the offered handshake, but Dev shook the other man's hand, his expression as impassive as the high rocky cliffs that surrounded them.

The man named Adam, oblivious, looked over Dev's shoulder and gave Emily a wave, too. "Hey. Nice day."

"Look," Landon's mom said, strolling over and putting a casual arm around Landon, "I didn't realize you were this far out in the middle of nowhere. Our ski group is meeting up in Vail. So do you mind if we just hang out here instead of going out and doing something?"

She was acting so casual and blasé about the chance to spend time with her son, as if she were a distant relative or a friend, not Landon's mom. Emily shouldn't judge—she didn't know the woman. But she'd lost her chance to hold her own child six years ago. Seeing Landon's mother reach out a hand for her boyfriend, even as she was supposed to be focused on her son, made Emily furious.

"Come on," the woman said, looking from the boyfriend to Landon and back again. "Let's hang out on the porch. Landon will get us something to drink."

To his credit, the outdoorsy boyfriend backed off, hands out. "I'll give you two some mother-son time. Do a little hiking around."

Relief was evident on Landon's face. Obviously, he wanted his mom to himself. "I'll show you my room and my school, Mom," he said, hugging her and holding on, his arms wrapped tightly around her.

She looked sad and happy at the same time, and some of Emily's anger drained away. It had to be hard to live two hours away from your child. Maybe the mother's distant attitude and focus on her boyfriend was an effort to protect her heart.

"How long can you stay, Mom?" Landon let go of her waist and grabbed her hand, clinging onto it with both hands, bouncing up and down.

"Oh, most of the day," she said. "If that's okay with your dad."

From behind him, Emily saw Dev square his shoulders. "That's fine," he said. "I'll just...give you a little space, too."

"Good idea," Landon's mom said promptly.

Adam opened the door of the SUV. "I'll drive over to the trailhead we passed on the way up," he said to Landon's mother. "Call me when you're ready to go."

He climbed in and roared off.

"Come on!" Landon tugged at his mother's hand, and they disappeared into Dev's cabin.

Dev stood watching them and then turned back toward his truck. His shoulders sagged a little. He seemed surprised to see Emily still standing there.

She couldn't help it; she was concerned. "Are you okay?" she asked him bluntly.

"Ah, sure. Whatever works for them." Then he tilted his head to one side. "How about I drive you for a quick visit with your mom?"

The thought of spending two hours in the truck with Dev brought mingled horror and joy into Emily's heart. "Oh, Dev, you don't have to do that."

He lifted his hands, palms up. "I've got nowhere else to go, and your car's not working. I'm in the way here."

"Don't you want to stick around in case Landon needs you?"

He shrugged. "Kind of, but he's with his mom. He's probably safer here with her than driving around somewhere."

"Oh, well…" The chance to see her own mother trumped her worries. "If you're sure."

"I'd be glad to," he said. "Let's go."

She followed him to his truck and wondered, would a long drive with the handsome, mysterious handyman be an Easter blessing…or a big mistake?

Chapter Five

As they headed down the road toward Emily's mother's care home, Emily leaned back, enjoying the chance to take in the scenery rather than worrying about her temperamental car. To the right, the mountains stood like giants pushing up the sky. Here in the broad valley, morning sunshine cast a glow over the fields. Herds of cattle clustered along the foothills, seeming to need togetherness in the vastness of the land.

There was almost no traffic, and Emily felt like she and Dev were alone in the world. She'd even left Lady at home when she'd noticed the dog wasn't feeling well; Lady had a finicky stomach, and she didn't want to put her through the long day of driving and sitting quietly at the care home.

Dev had turned up the heat when they'd gotten in, and now she was warm enough that she started to slip off her sweater. And then a wave of self-consciousness hit her; he'd see her scars, up close and personal. A messy-looking red-and-white patchwork up and down both arms, a reminder of the night she'd dragged her mother from the fire that had ruined both of their lives.

There was plastic surgery that could help, but it was considered cosmetic, and she wouldn't spend that kind of money on such a vain thing, even if she had it to spend. She'd pay for her mother to have surgery sooner than she'd have it herself, and that wasn't happening. But what did it matter if Dev saw? Let him recoil in horror. She slid off her sweater and held it in her lap, her face warming.

But he didn't seem to notice. "Sorry if the scene back there made you uncomfortable. Landon really misses his mom, so the idea that she was coming to see him got him excited. It just didn't play out quite the way we'd discussed."

"It's nice she came to see him."

Dev let out a snort. "She *came* up into the mountains to ski. Landon's just a side trip."

He sounded bitter, and she couldn't blame him if what he'd said was true. "It did seem that way, a little. Are you… Do you get along? Was it a hostile breakup?"

He took a hand off the steering wheel, flattened it and tilted it from side to side. "Somewhat. She cheated, I took her back, she did it again. Lots of door slamming and yelling." He glanced over at her. "Not that unusual of a story, but it was hard on Landon. He was three when the worst of it started, five when we split for good."

"And she got custody?"

He hesitated. "She did, at first. I'm not…" He blew out a breath. "I'm not the smartest when it comes to legal stuff, and she was seeing a lawyer for a while, so…yeah."

"But she let you have custody now, right?"

He nodded. "She wanted custody, initially, to win out over me. And because of how it would look if she *didn't* have custody. But the truth is, she wants a fun lifestyle more than a family one."

Emily's heart ached for Landon and, just a little bit, for the rugged man beside her. His jaw was square, his expression revealing no emotion, but Emily had the feeling there was a world of pain behind his simple words.

The lines that fanned out from the corners of his eyes bespoke a level of experience that she shared. This man hadn't had it easy. He was a book that grabbed her attention, one she'd like to read.

But she ought to know better. Aside from the

fact that he was out-of-her-league handsome, she'd already had her chance at a family, and she'd blown it. No way did she deserve another try.

She'd leave it at friendship, because it seemed like Dev needed a friend. No matter that she felt tempted to break her own rules and explore further.

How could any woman have chosen someone else over Dev? Not only was Dev handsome, but he had a thoughtful nature and a big heart full of love for his son.

"My life's not very interesting," he said. "What about you? Any sad love stories in your past?"

His words pulled her back from thinking about Dev as a romantic partner. What business did she have doing that? She bit her lip and stared out at the distant mountain peaks.

He'd told her about his past, and she ought to reciprocate by telling him something about hers. She'd gone through a fair amount of therapy after the fire, and one of the key takeaways was that keeping secrets kept you from healing.

"I'm a widow," she said, and held up a hand to halt his automatic expression of sympathy. "But before you feel all sorry for me, when I lost my husband, we were on the rocks." Then she felt bad for saying it. "Which doesn't mean it wasn't horrible to lose him. He had a family, parents who loved him and are still devastated by the fact that he died." And they blamed Emily for his death, still. "His life was cut short, and no matter the issues in our marriage, it was a terribly, terribly sad thing."

He nodded. "It can be tough to lose someone when you have unresolved issues," he said. "Me and Roxy, at least we can fight it out and get over it. When someone dies, you lose that chance."

"That's true." She'd wanted to rage at Mitch for being too drunk to stay awake and protect their son, but he'd paid the ultimate price. She couldn't find a focus for her anger, couldn't easily purge it.

She also couldn't bring herself to mention the loss of her son to Dev, but that was okay. A little at a time.

They rode along in silence that felt companionable, listened to music, pointed out features of the scenery. Finally, they got close to Mom's care home. "That's the turn, just up ahead." She pointed at the wooden sign that marked the home's long driveway.

Their conversation and Dev's company had distracted her, but now her stomach twisted into the usual knot that came from seeing her mother. It was compounded by the idea of Dev meeting her as well. Mom wasn't easy to be with now, even for Emily, who loved her.

"You don't have to come in," she said as they pulled into the parking lot. "I mean, you're welcome to, if you want. You could at least have Easter dinner with the group. They always have plenty of food. Although…don't get your expectations up too high. It's not exactly gourmet food."

"A little bland? Most places like this don't exactly pile on the spices."

"Exactly. Bland and easy to chew." She wrinkled her nose. "Still, the price of the meal is right, and we don't have to wash the dishes."

"Sounds good to me."

He pulled into a parking space by the side of the low-slung stone building. When he started to climb out, she put a hand on his arm to get his attention. "Mom has good and bad days," she said. "On bad days, she can be tough to be around."

His eyes crinkled, and he put his hand over hers and rubbed. "That's got to be hard," he said. "It's up to you. I don't have to come in, but I can. Either way."

She couldn't let the man sit in his truck for two hours after he'd been kind enough to drive her here. And she had to admit, it would be nice to have some companionship, not to face Mom and her issues alone. "Come on in," she said. "Welcome to my world."

Dev followed Emily into the care home. The woman was a puzzle, and though he shouldn't let himself get too interested in solving it—solving *her*—he found her hard to resist.

Her mom couldn't be very old, so she must have some condition or illness. Put that together with the fact that Emily was a widow who'd had a bad marriage, and his view of the smart, educated reading teacher with the perfect life was undergoing a change.

As soon as they reached the lobby, a woman in scrubs hurried over. "Hey, Emily. Your mom got upset this morning, and we felt like bringing her down to the group meal might upset her more. We can try it, now that you're here, or serve her lunch in her room."

Emily's forehead wrinkled. "Better serve her in her room. We'll keep her company while she eats."

"Want me to bring down a tray for you and your...friend?" She looked at Dev with frank interest, the type that told him Emily didn't often bring men to visit her mom.

That satisfied him way more than it should.

"That would be great, Abby. Thanks." She turned toward one of the hallways and then looked back at Dev. "You may not want to stay. She can get pretty agitated when she's confused or has some memories. It's one of the features of her condition." She must have seen his curious expression, because she added, "She has dementia. Probably early-onset Alzheimer's, although that's hard to diagnose."

"Whoa." Her matter-of-fact tone told him she'd been dealing with this for a while. "She's young, and you're young, to be dealing with that."

"Yeah. She's fifty-eight."

"Do you have other family?"

She shook her head. "Nope, Mom and I are it."

He got that, since his own family was untraditional, but he did have a pretty big network of cousins and former foster siblings. For her to be bearing this alone—not only the emotional pain of it, but the financial burden of care—that had to be tough.

But Emily's face told him that pity, or even an expression of sympathy, wouldn't be welcome right now. "I'll be interested to meet her."

She looked skeptical. "If you're sure."

"I'm sticking with you. At least I'll walk in there and make sure you're both okay. If it upsets her for me to stay, then I'll go wait in the truck."

"Thanks." She led the way down a hallway and pushed open a door with a flowered wreath on it.

They walked into a simple but pretty room, decorated with a homey comforter and curtains, nature pictures on the walls. The hospital bed was moved to a sitting-up position, and an attendant sat talking to the woman in the bed.

A woman who looked just enough like Emily to be haunting. She had the same auburn hair, though streaked through with gray, the same wide, expressive eyes.

But while Emily had scars only on her arms, this woman had scars over every visible part of her body.

The woman looked up and saw Emily and immediately pushed away the attendant. "I know her. That's my sister Andrea."

"Mom, it's Emily," she said. "Your daughter." She walked over, kissed the woman's cheek and sat down beside her. "Happy Easter."

"Easter!" The woman looked around, eyes wide and eyebrows raised high. "It's not Easter."

"It is, Mom. Are you ready for lunch? They're going to bring us in a couple of trays."

"I'm not hungry." She studied Emily. "I know you from a fire."

Emily's smile seemed to wobble. "You know me because I'm your daughter."

"I'm sorry about the fire. I fell asleep." She looked around wildly. "Where's James?"

Emily's face cramped with pain. "It's okay, Mom. I know you didn't mean to cause the fire."

"Where is he?" She tried to climb out of the bed.

The attendant, who'd moved to stand against the wall, came back over. "Miss Annette, you need to ask for help if you want to get out of bed."

Curiosity flared in Dev. Who was James?

Emily's mother sank back against the headboard and looked around again, and this time, she seemed to see Dev and focus on him. "Who is that man?"

"Mom, this is Dev. He's my friend, and he was kind enough to drive me here to see you."

Dev walked forward, slowly so as not to distress the woman. He also didn't hold out his hand to shake, figuring the sight of a big male hand might make her uncomfortable. "It's nice to meet you. Happy Easter."

She shook her head, staring at him. "I know why you're here. You're here to investigate."

"Nope, I'm not," he said. "I'm just a friend."

"You're here to see if I set the fire or if Mitch did. But we didn't. Not on purpose." She picked at the covers on the bed. "You have to be careful when you're cooking. I know that, Officer."

Dev blew out a breath, sympathy for Emily filling his heart. He wished he could help but just didn't know how.

Emily caught his eyes and shook her head a little. "Mom, Dev is going to wait outside. He's just a friend who gave me a ride."

"It was nice to meet you," he said and walked out to the sound of her mother's voice rising in what sounded like questions.

It put a different perspective on Emily's life, that was for sure.

As he passed the office, he overheard two women arguing. "Leave her alone," one was saying. "It's Easter."

"She needs to get going on this payment plan. We're working today—she can work, too." They saw him and lowered their voices, leading Dev to think they were talking about Emily.

Dev was starting to see that Emily's life was complicated. Bad enough to have a mother—your only family—in that condition. Having money problems piled on top of that seemed like too much.

He walked out of the building and crossed the parking lot slowly, thinking. This place was expensive; you could tell from how clean it was and how much personal attention the residents seemed to get.

But Emily no doubt was struggling to pay for

it on a teacher's salary. Even if her mother received some kind of benefits or had insurance, it wasn't likely to be enough to cover a place like this.

Was there any way he could help?

And then it came to him, as suddenly as the storms rose over the mountains.

He'd been stalling on the request for tutoring, but it was time to take action. Having her tutor Landon would help solve her problems and his, both.

The fact that it might require them to spend more time together was a concern, yes. The more time he spent with Emily, the more interesting she became to him.

But her situation seemed pretty dire, and that trumped any discomfort he might feel.

When Emily emerged from the care center an hour later, dark semicircles of fatigue showed under her eyes, and strands of hair escaped her ponytail. It almost looked like she'd been in a fight, and maybe, in some sense, she had.

"Did the nursing administrator find you?" He hated to ask.

She nodded. "Nothing I didn't know about, but it's become a little more urgent. The money situation, I mean."

"Come on, let's go," he said. "We can pick up

a pizza when we get close to home. I have the feeling you didn't eat much Easter dinner, and I also have a guess that Landon's mom isn't cooking him one. I doubt she even made him a peanut butter sandwich."

They climbed into the truck and drove a good ten minutes before she spoke. "Thank you for bringing me. I'm sorry you had to witness all that in there."

"I'm sorry you have to deal with that. It must be hard, seeing your mom that way."

She nodded. "It is. Mom never was perfect, but she loved to read and was a very smart woman. I got my interest in books and libraries from her. And now she can't read or understand anything."

"That's rough," Dev said, even as he was thinking, *It's all about the books with Emily, all about reading.*

As they drove along, he decided it was time to bring up his idea. "Listen, Emily, I've been thinking. Would you consider tutoring Landon after school?"

"Would I consider… Why, Dev?"

"He's not doing well in his academic subjects. They're suggesting that he repeat the third grade, and I really don't want that to happen. He'll be too big and old."

"Do they think tutoring is the answer?"

"Part of it, anyway." He didn't add that tutoring was the only part likely to work, since he himself wasn't able to work with Landon, who'd surpassed Dev's own reading ability last year.

"Hmm, I'll have to think about that," she said. "I need to get a second job to pay for Mom's care, so I won't have a lot of time."

"You don't understand. I'm not asking you to do it for free, I'm offering to pay you. For this to *be* your second job."

Her mouth twisted to one side, and she shook her head. "I need to make some real money, I'm afraid."

"How much do you need?" What she didn't know was that he had a significant nest egg. He'd been saving even before the divorce and more since then, scrimping on clothing for himself, cooking at home, taking advantage of free entertainment. He had earmarked the money for Landon's college education, but the first step was to get him through school and into college—which was less likely to happen if he failed third grade.

"Most private tutors make..." She googled on her phone. "Anywhere from twenty-five to eighty dollars per hour."

"I'll pay you the top end of the range," he said immediately. "And I'd like to start with five hours per week."

She stared at him. "That would basically solve all my money problems, but how..."

"How can I afford it?" He looked over at her. "I'm better off than I appear. Not exactly the millionaire next door, but I've done okay."

"I didn't mean to imply... It's just, I'd like to work for you for less. You've been so kind to me."

"There's no need to work for less. What do you think about taking the job?" He wanted her to do it, wanted to win her time in the same way he wanted to win every softball game he played. He should act neutral, leave it up to her, give her time to consider her situation and interests.

But Landon needed help now, and while she was trapped in the truck with him was probably the best time to make his case. "Landon's touchy, but he knows and likes you. And I've watched you teach. I can tell you're good at it and you care about the kids. You even live next door to us, so you could work with him after school without either of us having to drive anywhere. To me, it seems ideal. Will you do it?"

"I... Well, I'd love to work with Landon. He's a good kid. And the salary would be a huge help."

"Is that a yes?"

She chewed her lower lip, and he had to grip

the steering wheel to keep himself from reaching out to her. To what end, he wasn't quite sure.

"I… Maybe? Let me think about it a little bit."

"Of course." Again, there was the totally inappropriate urge to reach out to her.

He pulled into the pizza joint a few miles from the school, went in and ordered a pizza, then he came back out. He'd parked in the shade on the edge of the nearly empty parking lot.

"Twenty to thirty minutes," he said, climbing back into the truck. "Should have called ahead."

"I don't mind waiting. Dev, I've decided for sure. I'd love to work with Landon."

He did a fist pump. "Yes!"

She smiled at him. "And I'm so happy to have my money problems solved. You've made a huge difference in my life today. Thank you."

She reached for him and squeezed his shoulder. Could he be blamed for reaching up and touching her hand? And once he'd touched it, holding on?

He was just so grateful to her, as if he were the parent of a seriously ill child who'd just been given the medicine that could heal him. He was paying for her services, paying a lot, so he shouldn't feel beholden. A better man would look at this as a simple business transaction, beneficial to all parties, impersonal.

But few enough things in Dev's life had

worked out so easily and well. He looked out at the mountains, rising up behind the little pizza place, and this time, they made him feel more than hopeful. They made him feel that God knew what He was doing.

He looked over to say something to that effect and saw that she was watching him. Watching him closely.

He still had his hand on top of hers. All of a sudden, the air in the truck seemed thicker. "Your hair's a mess," he said, reaching over with his other hand to straighten out a strand that had fallen in front of her eyes.

"I... I've had a rough day." She was looking at him, her lips full and maybe trembling a little. She wasn't pulling away.

He was ready to lean forward to kiss her, and from the looks of things, she was going to let him. And then reality slapped him in the face.

He'd possibly ruin Landon's tutoring if he started up something with Emily. Because whatever he started, he couldn't finish it. No way could there be a relationship between someone as smart as Emily and someone like him.

He pulled his hand back, cleared his throat. "Better check on that pizza," he said, making his voice hearty and friendly and unromantic. And then he nearly flung himself out of the truck.

How involved did a parent have to be in his

child's tutoring? Because he was getting the feeling he'd better keep a safe distance from the reading teacher with the pretty brown eyes.

When they got back, Landon was sitting outside the cabin on the porch, alone.

Dev slammed on the brakes, jumped out of the truck and strode over. "Hey. Where's Mom?"

"S-s-she left." Landon was trying hard not to cry, Dev could tell, but there were tear tracks on his face.

Dev sat down next to Landon and put an arm around him, consciously unclenching his fists. She'd had less than a day with her son; did she have to leave early? Leave an eight-year-old alone? "How long ago?" he asked when he was sure he could govern his voice.

"A long time ago," he said. "She said she told you she had to leave after lunch."

Dev felt like the veins in his head were going to explode. She *hadn't* told him any such thing. But that was Roxy. She never took responsibility for her own omissions and mistakes.

And Dev was left in the position of either looking like a jerk himself, for not remembering what Roxy had told him, or making Roxy look like a liar. "We must have mixed up our signals," he managed to grit out, compromising.

Making them both look bad.

Emily had looked over at them, but she'd seemed to discern that Landon was okay and her presence wasn't needed. She'd gone into her cabin, and now she reemerged, letting Lady out to do her business.

"Lady!" Landon stood, then looked back at Dev. "Can I pet her?"

"If Ms. Carver says it's okay."

"Mom left a note," Landon called over his shoulder.

Dev did clench his fists at that. Roxy knew he wouldn't be able to read it. Oh, he'd try, sit down with a smartphone and puzzle out the letters in her messy handwriting, put them together and get the computer to speak the message. It would take all evening, but he'd do it.

Being with Emily all day, though, made Roxy's meanness stand out in stark contrast. Leaving him a written note, rather than a text he'd get right away and that he could have his phone read to him…it was just a way to torture him, to make excuses for her own behavior and then escape before he could call her on it.

She just plain stunk as a mother and as a co-parent. It was on him to make it up to Landon.

Starting with hiring him an excellent tutor, and then making sure he didn't do anything to spoil the friendly, professional connection between them.

Chapter Six

❧

They got started on tutoring right away, and Emily was mostly glad. Landon needed the help, and she needed the money.

But the first session had mixed results.

For one thing, it took place at the kitchen table in Landon and Dev's cabin, and Dev was there, moving in and out of the kitchen, putting on a pot of pasta for dinner, chopping onions, browning beef.

For another, Landon didn't want to be tutored. "I just sat around in school all day," he grumbled, even though she and Dev had arranged that he'd have an hour to be active and play before sitting down to his schoolwork. "I don't need tutoring."

"Yes, you do," Dev said without turning around. "I heard about your social studies test score. Even lower than the last one."

Landon's face, turned away from his father's, screwed up into a scowl.

"Tell you what," Emily said. "Let's talk about what's hardest in school, and what you like the best. That'll help me to plan lessons for you."

"It's all hard." Landon stared out the window, his shoe scuffing against the floor, his shoulders slumped. "I like outdoor time best."

Her heart went out to the child. Being behind in school was tough on a kid—tough on his ego, tough socially. The good news was that at Bright Tomorrows, lots of the kids struggled with academic problems. Landon wouldn't stand out as much as at a regular school. "Okay," she said. "What subject are you most worried about? What makes you feel most upset or unhappy, in the school day?"

Landon shrugged. "All of them."

Emily studied him, sending up a prayer that her creative teacher brain could come up with a way to reach this child. Even though he was acting indifferent, if not defiant, she could see through the facade to a discouraged child who didn't know how to break out of the cycle of failure.

At their feet, Lady shifted and sighed. Landon looked down, and for the first time, his expression lifted. "Can I pet her?"

There it was, the breakthrough idea she'd

hoped for. "Yes, in a minute. First, I'm going to write down four words, and you tell me if you can read any of them. Only one is easy." On her big notepad, with a marker, she wrote *dog, poodle mix, lady.* She held the tablet out to Landon.

He glanced over at them. His finger gravitated to the shortest word, one he probably recognized by shape. "D-o-g. Dog."

"Yes, very good. Want to try one of the others?" She was really just trying to assess his reading level, and she had her own idiosyncratic way of doing it, focused on a child's interests. Since Landon didn't want to talk about school subjects, it looked like her one for-certain winner was dogs.

He looked at the next-shortest word. "L-ah-dee," he tried. "Lad?" And then his face fell. "But there's a *y* at the end. Lad-why. That's not a word."

"You're close. Did you ever learn about the *y* at the end of some words, how it can sound like 'eee'?"

He shrugged.

"Try it. Sound it out, with the '*y* that's an eee' sound."

"Lad-eee. Lad-eee." He frowned, and then his eyes widened as he got it. "Lady!" he shouted.

At the sound of her name, Lady looked up, panting, and nuzzled Landon. It was the perfect reinforcement. "Look, I can read your name," he told the dog, and he pointed to the word *Lady* as if the dog could learn to read it, as well.

"She's smart, but she's not that smart," Emily said. "Can you find her name on her tag?"

He knelt immediately, and Lady patiently allowed him to fumble with her collar. Landon did indeed find the word. They went on from there, figuring out "poodle mix," and then looking at other words that had the *y* or the *le* ending, until Landon started to get frustrated.

"English is hard," she said to him. "You're doing well."

"Español es mas fácil?" Dev said, making it sound like a question.

She'd almost forgotten Dev was there, and now she realized he'd been staying quiet and out of the way. *"Si*, it's easier to read. Do you read Spanish?"

He got a funny look on his face and then shook his head. "No, I never learned."

She shrugged. "You must have learned to speak it in the home, then," she said. "Rather than in a class, like I did."

"Yeah. A couple of the places I lived, Spanish was the main language. I had to learn enough to get by."

She studied him. "Places you lived?"

He nodded, added salt to the pasta sauce and tasted it.

"Military family?"

He shook his head. "I grew up in foster care. Lived in a few different homes."

"Eleven!" Landon said from where he lay on the floor, waving a toy in front of Lady's long nose. "Dad lived with eleven different families when he was a kid." He said it like it was some kind of achievement.

Emily looked quickly at Dev and caught the slightest pinch in his expression before he smiled. "Everybody's a record setter in some way or other."

"Sounds rough."

"It was at times, but hey. I learned Spanish and I learned to cook." He used a garlic press to squeeze garlic into a bowl of soft butter, stirred it and then spread it on a split-open loaf of Italian bread.

She leaned back, watching him.

Curiosity about this man who could make the best of a difficult childhood—and who actually owned a garlic press—flashed through her, warm and intense. She didn't want to be nosy, shouldn't be. His childhood wasn't her business, and she ought to be polite and drop the subject.

But this man and his son tugged at her. The more she learned about them, the more she felt for them. And maybe part of it was to do with Landon, with his being the same age her son would have been, but that wasn't all of it. They were a fascinating pair. They'd come through some challenges, Dev with his childhood and both of them with a divorce, and yet they were still positive. She really wanted to know how, what their secret was. "Did you grow up in the Denver area, or all over?"

"Denver and the farm country around it." He slid the bread into the oven. "How about you?"

"Just a few towns over on the other side of the mountain." Indeed, she'd spent most of her life, including her married life, in this part of the state.

He didn't volunteer any more information about himself and Landon, so she didn't press. Instead, she leaned down and showed Landon Lady's favorite spot to be scratched, right behind the ears. Now that they weren't working anymore, he was talkative and happy, asking her a million questions about the dog.

It was hard to leave the kitchen, cozy and warm, infused with the fragrances of garlic and tomato and bread. Her quiet home and the can of soup she'd likely heat up for dinner both seemed lonely after being here. But she had her own life and couldn't mooch off theirs. "I'd better let you men get on with your dinner," she said and started gathering up her books.

"You want to stay?" Dev asked.

The question, hanging in the air, ignited danger flares in her mind.

The answer was obvious: yes, she did want to stay. But an *Unwise! Unwise!* warning message seemed to flash in her head.

Spending even more time with Dev and Landon was no way to keep the distance she knew she had to keep. As appealing as this pair was, she couldn't risk getting closer. Her heart might not survive the wrenching away that would have to happen, sooner rather than later.

She fumbled with her book bag, reluctant to give the answer she knew she had to give.

Now, why had he gone and invited Emily to dinner?

It was bad enough to have the pretty reading teacher in his kitchen for the after-school hour, talking with and teasing and *teaching* Landon, getting more thinking and work out of him than Dev ever could've.

If she joined them for dinner, he and Landon would both start to get attached. And that was exactly what they couldn't do. They were her clients. Landon was her student. It was important that things stay at that same simple, professional level.

"It's a really nice offer, but I shouldn't stay." She stuffed the rest of her books and papers into a huge tote bag.

Relief and disappointment wrestled inside him. "That's fine. It was just a thought."

"Stay, Ms. Carver. I want to keep playing with Lady." Landon looked up at her. "I'll walk her for you after dinner."

"Ms. Carver needs to get home," Dev said, wishing it weren't so.

"Please? I worked really hard today." His eager face looked pleadingly from one adult to the other, his arm wrapped around Lady.

Emily glanced over at Dev, her expression amused, reflecting the way he felt. Manipulation. Kids were such pros at it. But who could say no to that face, those eyes?

She must have seen that he was caving. "Well," she said, "that garlic bread *does* smell really good."

"Yes!" Landon pumped his arm. "You'll love it. Dad's garlic bread is the best."

She smiled. "How could I turn that down?"

Dev's heart was light as he spooned spaghetti and sauce onto plates. Emily filled water glasses at his direction, and Landon got out the silverware and napkins. At the table, they held hands and prayed before digging in.

It could have been awkward—they didn't know each other well, and there *had* been that weird moment in the truck, when he'd gotten so tempted to pull her close—but Landon and Lady kept things light. Lady scarfed down a crust of bread that got knocked to the floor, so quickly that they all laughed. Landon talked about some of the boys in his classes in a way that suggested he was starting to make some decent friends. Which Dev was glad about but still wanted to keep an eye on, given that it was a school for troubled boys.

When they were clearing the dishes and Landon had gone into the front room to watch TV, Dev asked Emily about it. "Do you think there are kids here Landon should stay away from?"

She shook her head. "Not really. I don't know every boy's story, but I know if they've engaged in criminal behavior that's considered dangerous to others, they're not admitted. We're sort of midrange in terms of behavior issues."

He nodded, filling the sink with hot water, squirting in dish soap. "I guess from the outside, any kid's issues can look bad, including Landon's. I know he's not going to set another fire, but that's not obvious to everyone."

"He seems like a gentle kid." She brought over the rest of the dishes. "That's true of most of the kids here. Half of the trouble is that they didn't get the help they needed in school, and they fell behind and got frustrated."

"I hear that," he said, letting too much feeling leak into his voice.

And then he wished he hadn't, because her eyes darkened with sympathy. "It must have been tough living with all those different families, especially if it involved changing schools a lot, too."

He nodded and busied himself scrubbing the pan he'd used to brown the beef.

"Did you struggle in school?"

A flash of remembered frustration brought sweat to the back of his neck. Every school he'd attended had been at a different spot in the textbook. Every one had given different sorts of tests. And had different expectations of behavior.

He'd gotten assigned to low-level reading classes, and once he'd been pulled out of class for special help with reading. But just as he'd started to connect with the teacher and learn, he'd gotten moved to another foster home, another district. And the process of failing had started all over again.

He'd envied the kids comfortable enough

in the classroom to joke around, the ones who could sneak a handheld game under their desk or pass notes and still manage to find their place in the book or come up with the right answer when the teacher called on them. Emily had probably been that kind of kid, though he already knew her well enough to speculate that she was more likely to have sneaked an unauthorized book to read than played video games or passed notes.

And that was just a reminder of why she wasn't for him. "Listen," he said without answering her question, "I know you have things to do back at your place. I'll finish up here." He hated his own tone, abrupt, ungracious.

She'd been smiling, looking sympathetic, but at his rude dismissal, the smile slid off her face. "Oh, sure, okay," she said. She dried her hands without looking at him again, grabbed her bag, snapped her fingers to get Lady to her side. "See you in school tomorrow, Landon," she said, and she disappeared out the door before he could feel more than a pang of regret that he'd hurt her feelings by pushing her away.

Keeping his reading inadequacy a secret was going to be harder and harder the more Emily Carver infiltrated their lives.

Chapter Seven

On the Friday after she started tutoring Landon, Emily headed toward the group of students and staff clustered outside the school building with a firm goal: *not* to be assigned to the same hiking group as Dev and Landon.

It was Earth Day, and the school had taken advantage of the good weather with an outdoor activity—an all-day, all-school hike.

"Everyone listen up," Ashley Green called over the talking and laughing of students excited to be let out of class. She wore casual shorts and a Bright Tomorrows T-shirt, her hair in a simple ponytail instead of its usual neat bun, and Emily realized, with surprise, that she was pretty. She seemed less intimidating than usual, as well. Ashley was relatively new at Bright Tomorrows and didn't seem to have many friends yet. For the first time, Emily realized she ought to reach out to the woman, despite the fact that Ashley was her boss.

"Two rules," Ashley continued when everyone had quieted down. "No one hikes alone, which means you have to keep a lookout for slower members of your group. Don't keep going if they're falling behind. And rule number two, every student has to have an adult in sight at all times."

"Aw, they aren't much to look at," one of the older students yelled, earning glares from the adults and laughter from the students.

Ashley laughed, too, but then her face got serious. "It's no joke, Byron. Hiking in the Colorado mountains always has an element of risk. We've assigned someone trained in first aid and someone experienced with maps and compasses to each group, but everyone needs to have their wits about them."

So the groups were already assigned. It made sense. Emily looked across the crowd and spotted Landon and Dev. Of course they were already here; she'd waited until they were out of sight before leaving her cabin.

It was what she'd done the whole week since their first tutoring session, when Dev had invited her to share their cozy meal and then kicked her out.

The man was good to look at, as Hayley kept

saying. Interesting, too, with a kindhearted side. A good dad. She couldn't deny that she felt a spark when she spent time around him.

Maybe he sensed it, and that was why he'd pushed her away. He was way out of her league lookswise, that was for sure.

But even if he'd looked more ordinary, like she did, nothing was going to happen between them. No-thing. Nothing. Emily didn't do relationships, not anymore.

Funny how often she was having to remind herself of that these days.

It was just that this was the first time she'd found a man appealing since she'd become a widow. It didn't mean anything special. She just needed to ride it out and take care of herself so the awareness of all she'd lost and all she couldn't have didn't start her on a downward spiral.

She couldn't drag her own heart and her ticking biological clock through the mud of a doomed attraction. So she'd suggested that Landon meet her in the library for tutoring one day, and in her own kitchen the next.

The tutoring sessions had been okay. It was early times, and she was still assessing his status at the same time she helped him with his immediate issues. She'd sent an email to Dev, copying Ashley and recommending that Landon be tested for dyslexia by a licensed educational psychologist. Meanwhile, she'd worked with him on a test review, and she was pretty confident that Landon had passed the test, so that was something.

On the other hand, he had trouble sitting still and got frustrated easily. She had her hands full trying to keep him on task and engaged after a full day of being in class. So ADHD was something they should also keep in mind, but she wasn't going to dump all that on Dev and Landon at once.

Today's excursion would be good for Landon, a chance to burn off some energy and find out what the Colorado mountains were really like, since she'd guessed from things he'd said that he hadn't had much time out in nature when he'd lived with his mom in Denver.

It was also a chance for him to feel like a part of things, rather than the new kid with the reading problems.

She'd like to see Landon discover the thrill of reaching the top of a mountain under his own steam.

"Have they assigned groups yet?" Hayley rushed over from the kitchen door.

"Not yet. Or rather, they've assigned them, but they haven't told us yet. You get to go?"

"I'd better. I'm grilling the hot dogs. Listen

for my name, will you? I have to grab my hiking boots."

"Sure will. Hope we're together."

But it turned out they weren't. Instead, she learned that Landon had begged to be in the same group as Emily and Lady, and whoever had assigned the groups had given in. So he and Dev clustered with Emily and the other members of their group of ten, waiting for further instructions. The other two adults in Emily's group were Stan Davidson, the math teacher, and Maria, from the counseling department, whom Stan seemed intent on impressing.

"To make things fun," Ashley said, "we're going to race to the lake at the top of the trail."

"Yeah, let's go!" one of the boys said. Others pumped arms in the air, and two actually started running for the trailhead.

"Whoa. Stay here, guys. It's not that kind of race—it's a timed race. Each group will take off ten minutes apart, and we'll see who reaches the lake in the least amount of time based on their start."

Emily had participated in these challenges before, but being with the kids in the gorgeous Rockies never got old.

Being with Dev, though, was going to be more of a challenge. She gave him a little smile, but he didn't return it. Maybe it was because he was focused on checking Landon's knapsack.

Or maybe he just wanted to keep his distance.

Which was a good thing, she reminded herself, even though it didn't feel that way.

Their group was second, and the kids rushed ahead. Stan gave a loud whistle. "Remember the rules," he yelled. "Adults in sight all the time."

"And pace yourselves," Emily called out. "If you start too fast, you'll get tired and hit a wall."

The kids waved and yelled their agreement and hurried ahead anyway. But when they started around a bend, they stopped and waited until the rest of the group caught up.

Emily tried to talk to Stan, but he made it obvious her presence was unwelcome as he bragged to the pretty school counselor about his professional successes prior to coming to Bright Tomorrows. Dev was bringing up the rear, so Emily quickened her pace and reached the kids in the front of the group.

After just a few minutes of climbing, it wasn't hard to keep up, because the kids had slowed way down. Everyone was short of breath.

They crossed a rushing, icy stream on a double-plank bridge. Surrounding them were pines and, beyond those, peaks capped and lined with snow. The ground was rough and the trail faint, and when the kids made a wrong turn, Emily called out and reminded them to look for the cairns—little stacks of rocks—that stood in for signs for much of the way.

She took deep breaths of the cool air and listened to the sound of water on rocks, mingled with kids' voices and the caws of bright blue Steller's jays. The path curved onto the edge of a drop-off and then climbed higher.

Some of the kids moved faster, and when they shouted, Emily hurried to find out what was wrong. But the boys were all whooping and jumping around at a spot where the trail opened out onto a wide, nearly flat field covered in white. "It's snow!" one of the newer boys yelled.

It was no surprise to Emily that the snowpack remained in April, but it was a delight to the kids. They ran and slid along the snowfield and then picked up the path again on the other side.

The boys were getting excited as they climbed higher, wanting to be the winning team, and the other adults dawdled behind her, almost out of sight. Emily was thankful for Lady, trotting along beside her. She'd taken off Lady's service dog vest and put her on a long leash so she could sniff and dodge back and forth across the trail like any other dog. Lady still checked in with her frequently, though, looking up, panting, seeming to smile.

She was a good companion. Better than another person. Especially a person like Dev. Sure, he was good-looking—very—and a good guy overall, but the way he ran hot and cold would be tough on any woman he dated.

Did he date anyone? It was hard to imagine he'd already met someone in Little Mesa or at the school, but maybe he'd left a hometown sweetheart behind in Denver.

Deliberately, she pushed thoughts of the handyman out of her mind and focused on the wind in the trees and the sunshine sparkling on the little stream that ran beside the trail. It was so beautiful here, so easy to see God at work, the artistry of His creation. She prayed without words, feeling gratitude for all God's blessings. He'd brought her joy out of pain. No, she'd never forget the awful things that had happened to her, that she'd caused, but with God's help, she'd built a life where she could be of service. She loved her work; she had friends; she lived in a beautiful place. That was a lot to be thankful for.

Most of the group had continued hurrying ahead, waiting impatiently whenever a bend in the trail threatened to put the lagging hikers out of sight. But Landon had fallen behind the other boys, and now he sat on a rock beside the trail, breathing hard. Another boy was with him.

"Taking a rest?" Emily asked as she reached them. She smiled her approval at the two boys. "Good for you, following the rules about how nobody should hike alone."

"This is hard," Landon complained between gasps.

"It's the altitude, dude," the other boy said. "You're not used to it."

"You're right. Hank, can you run up and get the other boys to stop? Landon isn't the only one who's not used to the altitude. We should all take a break, get some water and maybe some trail mix."

The mention of food wiped the protest off the two boys' faces. They wanted to win the challenge, but food was a bigger draw.

Stan and his prospective, way-too-young girlfriend came around the curve, and then Dev behind them.

"Anything wrong?" Dev asked, striding to Landon's side.

"I got tired." Landon's face was flushed, and he was still breathing hard.

"It's a good time for a break, anyway," Emily said. "The next section is tougher. We should all drink some water."

"We want to win," one of the boys said, scarfing down trail mix. "C'mon, let's go."

"We'll go ahead with the boys," Stan said,

gesturing to himself and Maria, "if you city folks want to stay back and take a slower pace." He glanced at Dev as he said it, then at Maria.

Emily rolled her eyes. Stan was trying to show off his manly hiking skills by putting down Landon and Dev as inferior.

Dev wouldn't be baited, however. "Good idea," he said easily. "This is a big group to keep all together."

"Can we win if they're not with us?" one of the boys asked.

"Yes, if the majority of our group is fast. It's the overall statistics of the thing." They headed off, Stan continuing to explain how the winners would be decided based on average time.

So Emily had to make a choice: she could stay back with Landon and Dev, or she could go forward, listen to a math lecture and get in the way of Stan's planned romance.

"Do you mind if I walk with you guys?" she asked Dev.

"Of course not," he said, his voice neutral.

"Walk with us!" Landon urged, and while she figured that his enthusiasm had more to do with Lady than with her, it still felt good.

They headed across a field of glacial rocks, and it was tough going. Landon even said he wanted to turn back, but Dev wouldn't allow it.

"We can go slow, but we need to get to the top. We committed to the hike, and we'll finish it."

Finally, they made it across the field and to a wooden sign, and since Landon was out of breath, they stopped beside it. "Can you read it?" Emily asked. "Look, trace the letters."

Dev frowned at her. "It's a day to be free from school."

But Landon was running his fingers along the carved wooden letters. "Lak-uh," he sounded out.

"Silent *e*," she reminded him.

"Lake!" He looked up at her. "Right?"

"Yep. Good job. Any guesses about what the first word says?" She covered up the second half.

He sounded out the first part easily. "Mag!"

"Exactly." She pulled her hand back from the rest of the word, and he shouted it out before she could offer help. "Magpie! Another silent *e*!"

"Really good job," she said, giving him a quick hug and then glancing up at Dev, afraid she'd been too hands-on with his son. But Dev stood looking at the sign, not at them. He was even running his fingers along the letters, the same way Landon had done.

He looked up, seemed to notice that she was watching him and backed away from the sign. "Might be making some new direction signs for the school," he said, flushing. "This is a nice design. We should get going."

"Sure," she said, wondering why he suddenly seemed uncomfortable. "It's about ten, fifteen minutes more to the top."

"You hear that, Landon? We're almost there."

They hiked quickly now and soon heard the sounds of the rest of the group. They came out of a strand of pines and stopped, all three of them staring at the vista before them.

The mountain peaks, snow-capped and majestic against the deep blue sky, formed a circle around the sparkling lake. Overhead, a couple of eagles swooped and soared. The air smelled crisp and piney, and the buzzy chirp of frogs sounded from a rushing creek that fed into the lake.

"Wow, cool!" Landon said.

Dev was looking around, nodding slowly. "Wow is right."

"Can we go swimming?" Landon asked.

Dev and Emily looked at each other, amused. "That's some cold water," Dev said. "Way too cold to swim in."

"I think you can even see some ice on it," Emily said.

"It's sure beautiful. I'm glad we came." Dev's tension finally seemed to have left him. They headed over and greeted the others, shucked off their backpacks, and then Dev, Emily, Landon and a couple of other boys from their team walked down to the lake. The boys stuck their hands into the water and, indeed, shrieked about how cold it was. The boys gathered ice shards and then, urged by Ashley as she passed by, collected sticks for a fire. Dev and Emily leaned on a large lakeside rock, admiring the scenery.

"We're not in Denver, that's for sure," Dev said. "You've hiked up here before?"

"Yes," she said, "but I still get thrilled every time."

"Wait a minute," Landon said, "did we win?" And the boys went running over to the rest of the group.

Leaving Emily to admire the view and the man beside her.

What would it be like to be a normal, carefree pair of people who were drawn to each other, who'd just taken a hike and now had a few minutes alone in a gorgeous place? What would it be like to let her gaze linger on Dev, rather than looking quickly away at the far mountains? What would it be like if instead of shivering alone, she moved closer to his warmth?

Those were questions she shouldn't be asking, but here, surrounded by God's beauty, she somehow couldn't stop herself.

* * *

Dev sucked in mountain air and studied the peaks and the lake. He was trying to keep his focus there instead of on Emily, but it wasn't easy.

There was no one he'd rather be with to see this wonder. He'd really tried to keep his distance, but being here, in God's beautiful creation, he just couldn't do it anymore.

Things like reading ability receded in importance next to all this splendor. Maybe he didn't have to feel so ashamed, didn't have to hide so much.

For sure, things like reading apps and text-to-voice technology seemed to reside in another world.

A breeze blew a strand of hair across Emily's face, and before he could stop himself, he brushed it back behind her ear.

She looked up at him, eyes wide.

Oh, did his hand want to linger, to cup that soft cheek, to drown in those warm, chocolate-colored eyes. He even moved an inch or two closer and noticed that she was shivering. "Are you cold?" he asked, starting to put an arm around her.

"Come and get it!" A loud call from behind them reminded Dev that he was in public. He stepped back.

"Guess we should go get our hot dogs before the boys eat them all," she said. Her voice sounded a little breathless.

"We should." He didn't put a hand on the small of her back as they headed toward the group, even though he wanted to. Wanted to a lot.

And wanting to touch her was the tip of the iceberg, because his feelings were starting to go deeper.

You can't even read the sign your son figured out. What would she think if she knew?

But maybe it wasn't so awful. Maybe she'd be understanding.

Maybe he could, real quick, learn to read at a decent adult level. He'd looked at those letters, traced them with his finger, and they'd clicked into place. Lake. Magpie Lake.

"Before we eat, we'll have a prayer," Ashley Green said. "Let's all hold hands in a circle and thank the Lord for His blessings."

That led to some grousing among boys who were squeamish about touching one another, but Ashley was firm, and so they all did it. Which meant he got to take Emily's hand in his.

He squeezed it a little, and she squeezed back, and then he scolded himself and tuned into the prayer. Ashley was kind of going on long with it, talking about how God who made everything didn't make mistakes, that everyone here was His perfect creation, accepted just as they were. "And we thank You for that acceptance, and promise to live up to it and be closer to the people You want us to be. Amen."

As the boys rushed to grab hot dogs from Hayley and her helper, and as they all sat around eating, Dev deliberately took a spot apart from Emily. His thoughts were reeling.

Was it true that God accepted everyone as they were—accepted him, even?

God was a father, the father of all. Dev's own father hadn't been there for him, so that connection of human fathers with God had never really jelled for Dev.

But now that he was a father, and an involved one, he was starting to understand the comparison. When Landon made mistakes or struggled, Dev didn't dislike or abandon him; he tried to help him and loved him just the same.

Maybe God loved Dev just the same, too, despite all his flaws and weaknesses.

Maybe— "Hey!" he yelled as something cold exploded against his back.

"Snowball fight!" Stan said. He lobbed another snowball, this one at Emily.

Dev wasn't going to take *that* sitting down. He jumped up and formed a couple of snowballs and beaned Stan good.

Then the boys were all in it, laughing and throwing wildly and acting not like delinquents or struggling students, but like kids.

Lady chased snowballs and then looked confused when they broke and melted in her mouth, making everyone laugh.

"We leave in half an hour," Ashley called. "You may want to rest a little. It's a long trip down."

"Good idea," Emily said, wiping sweat from her forehead and heading toward the backpacks.

Of course, the boys didn't pay the suggestion about resting a lot of attention, but Hayley went over and flopped down beside Emily, who was leaning back against her pack and…yeah. She was actually reading a book, some thick, serious-looking one.

Dev walked around picking up a few scraps of paper the kids had left, keeping an ear open to their discussion.

"What do you think of it so far?" Hayley was asking. "Do you love it as much as I did?"

"It's *so* good," Emily said. "I stayed up way too late last night. I'm at that part where the Nazis are coming into Paris, and they're hiding in that basement…"

They went on chattering about the book, and Dev listened for a couple of minutes and then headed down to the water. Even if he *did* learn to read better than he could now, he wasn't likely to ever get to the point of reading a big thick book like that. Didn't even know if he wanted to. He might prefer to just watch a TV show about World War II.

So did that mean he and Emily were incompatible?

"How are things going, Dev?" It was Ashley, who'd come up alongside him and now perched on a rock, inviting him to join her.

"Good. Great place." He gestured at their surroundings.

"It is." She studied him. "Is something wrong?"

"Well, I…" He hesitated. She looked so understanding. Maybe he could confide in her about his trouble with reading. Maybe she'd know how to help him, the way she knew how to help Landon.

But she was his boss. She might fire him if she realized he couldn't read the warning labels on the cleaning solutions he used, not without scanning them into his phone and using the text-to-voice program. Better to keep it all to himself.

"I'm fine," he said instead of talking to her about himself. "Did you know we got Emily to do some extra tutoring with Landon?"

"I heard. She had to clear it with me, since she's kind of moonlighting." She smiled at him.

"I'm sure Landon will catch up. It's just a matter of persistence and confidence, which I'm sure you can help him with. Anyone can learn."

"Yeah. Thanks." He watched her thoughtfully while she went off whistling for the kids to gather their things and start their downhill trek.

Anyone can learn. He knew that to be the case in many areas of life, but he just wasn't sure it was true about something so unnatural to him as reading.

Chapter Eight

❦

"You didn't have to do this." Dev leaned back in his chair the next Tuesday evening and gave a satisfied sigh. "But I'm glad you did. The beef stew was great."

"Yeah, thanks, Ms. Carver. Dad never makes stuff like that."

"You gotta love the Crock-pot," she said, waving away the compliments. And it *had* been easy, but she'd gone to a little extra trouble, browning the meat and onions first, making biscuits to go with the hearty stew. She was the first to admit she wasn't much of a cook, but she'd wanted to do something nice for Dev and Landon, wanted to please them.

Food was always pleasing to men, she knew that. Especially after a long day of work or school. And meat and potatoes, comfort food, were high on most males' lists.

"I wanted to thank you," she said. "You did me a big favor driving me to see Mom again on Sunday."

"We'll go every week if I can go to the arcade!" Landon was kneeling beside Lady, rubbing her belly. "Can we, Dad?"

"Oh, no, I wouldn't—" Emily started.

"Maybe not *every* Sunday—" Dev said at the same time.

They both laughed, and Emily hurried to get her comment in. "The mechanic thinks he'll have my car done this week, or next week at the latest." And thanks to the generous wage Dev had offered, she was able to put the repair on her credit card, knowing she'd be able to pay it off.

"It was fun," he said. And it had been. They'd turned up the radio and discovered that all three of them liked to sing along to country music. They'd stopped for pizza again on the way home.

It had felt like a family outing, and even though Emily's mom hadn't been very responsive, Emily had felt good when she'd gotten back home.

"Landon and I will do the dishes," Dev said.

Landon made a face.

"I have an idea," Emily said. "I have a new audiobook of a mystery story, and the book, too.

If Landon would want to listen to it, maybe he could do it while we clean up."

"Could I watch TV instead?" Landon asked.

"Good try, buddy, but no," Dev said. "It's reading or dishes."

"You can keep Lady company while you listen to the story." Emily smiled at Landon, glad she'd figured out the way to his heart—or, at least, to his cooperation.

"Okay," Landon said instantly, proving her right.

"But you do have to follow along. There are good pictures." Emily got Landon set up and then returned to the kitchen, where Dev was clearing dishes off the table. "I think he'll like this book," she said. "And this is a terrific way for him to improve his reading. I can let you borrow the materials."

"Good," he said. "I, uh, I sometimes listen to audiobooks myself. Nothing deep," he added, waving a hand. "Want me to wrap up these biscuits?"

"Sure." Emily indicated the drawer that held plastic bags and wrap, then pushed up her sleeves and turned on the water to fill the sink.

Dev bagged up the biscuits, then came to stand beside her. He touched her arm. "What are the scars from?"

She pulled away. Dev had been around her

more now, had seen the scars multiple times, and she'd forgotten to be self-conscious around him, until now.

He looked contrite. "Sorry. It's definitely not my business."

"No, it's okay. I... I was in a fire."

"Rough. Same fire as your mom?"

Emily drew in a breath and let it out, slowly, and nodded.

He nudged her aside and dunked dishes into the water. "Let me wash. You can dry. And you don't have to tell me, but I'm interested if you would want to. And I'm here if you just need to talk." He glanced at her, his eyes warm, his kindness obviously sincere.

"Ah, I... Thanks." How did he *do* that? How did he make her feel so very good and cared for? "It was just..." She swallowed and couldn't go on. Of course she couldn't. She couldn't tell him how awful she'd been or what she'd done.

He leaned a little closer, his arm touching hers. "Life stinks sometimes," he said. "Is the fire what made you need a service dog?"

She cleared her throat. "Yeah. I... I wasn't getting over it. Lady helps."

He moved behind her, put his hands on the backs of her shoulders and rubbed, gently. It felt like the perfect amount of warmth and pressure.

She let the pan she was drying slip to the counter and closed her eyes.

How had he guessed that she held her tension in her shoulders? And when was the last time anyone had touched her so sweetly, with the intent of comforting her?

All too soon he dropped his hands, stepping away.

Emily turned to him, her shoulders tingling where he'd rubbed them. Her face felt hot.

"Don't worry." He'd taken a couple of steps back. For the first time, she noticed how big he seemed in her little kitchen, and how masculine among the frilly curtains and flower centerpiece. "I won't make a habit of that. Just... I don't know how to make it better. I thought—" He broke off. "I don't want to stress you out more."

"Thanks." Emily walked over and peeked into the living room, saw that Landon had dozed off, using Lady as a pillow, the book open on his chest. The sight made her smile, made her feel tender inside.

But in the kitchen, there was still Dev to deal with, and her feelings for him were far more complicated. She couldn't think of anything to say to him. Because she couldn't blurt out that she liked the way he'd touched her, that no one else touched her so gently and kindly, could she?

"You've gotten past it." He leaned over the trash can and pulled the bag out, tied the drawstring, and over and above the fact that she still felt warm from his touch, she marveled at a man who would take the trash out without being nagged to do so.

"I'll take this out when we go." He walked over to the sink and washed his hands.

The kitchen felt so small. She was hyper-aware of him moving through it. He turned toward her, and everything in her yearned for him to take her in her arms, to hold her, make her feel that warmth and safety, that gentle tenderness, again and more.

Lady barked in the front room, probably at someone walking by on the road. Landon stirred.

"I should get Landon home," Dev said. "He's tired. He'll go right to bed." And then he put a hand on Emily's arm. "Come with me."

"What?"

He didn't look away. His eyes were on her, warm brown eyes, intense. His hand seemed to burn her shoulder. "I just want to be with you."

Her heart seemed to reach out of her chest toward him, so great was her yearning. She wanted to be with him, too. Only what did that mean?

He was still studying her, and she couldn't

quite recognize the look in his eyes. It was still kind, but there was an intensity there that she hadn't seen in him before, and it scared her.

Emily stepped back, confused. She wanted to be with Dev, too, longed for it. But she was pretty sure he didn't mean the same thing she did. "I've given you the wrong idea. I don't do that." It came out sounding prudish, and maybe he'd think she meant she wouldn't put herself into a potentially intimate situation with a man.

Which was true.

But what she'd really meant was, she didn't get to be close with a man like Dev, hadn't earned it, didn't deserve it. The scars on her arms were a daily witness to her failure.

Connecting with Dev was too enticing, making her long for things she couldn't have. "I'll see you at work," she said, and she deliberately moved away from him, starting to scrub her stove, which didn't need scrubbing.

He stood behind her for a minute, without speaking. She could hear his breathing, a little quickened, just like her own was.

"Right. Sorry. Landon, come on." He walked into the living room, and she heard him waking Landon, helping the sleepy boy gather his things. Then he gave her an impersonal wave, and they were gone.

Emily dropped the sponge and sank down

onto a kitchen chair, wrapping her arms around herself.

This was getting too dangerous. She was at risk of getting her heart entangled, and maybe Dev's, too. Worst of all, Landon's, if he was starting to think of her as a mother figure.

Her decision to stay away from relationships had seemed relatively easy up until now. Meeting Dev and Landon, though, had opened up a vista to her, as wide and free and beautiful as the view at Magpie Lake. It was a vista of a new life, a new family, motherhood, the love of a good man.

For the first time, she realized what she was throwing away when she turned her back on Dev and Landon. Her life seemed to stretch in front of her, lonely and empty and sad.

And she had absolutely no right to feel that way. She'd brought her situation on herself. Moreover, she had much to be grateful for. She ticked the positives in her life off on her fingers: her job, the kids, her friends, the natural beauty around her, her faith most of all. It was something she did regularly, at the suggestion of one of her counselors: focus on the positive. Think about all there was to be grateful for.

And she *was* grateful, truly. It was just that Dev and Landon were so special. She'd never meet anyone like them again.

She stood and walked over to her dish rack. Best to stay busy.

She reached for the clean plates and stopped. Her hand dropped back to her side.

She *liked* the look of that full dish rack, so different from her usual solo plate, cup and fork. Liked the look of having had people here. Almost like a family.

Her lower lip trembled, just a little. Lady stood, shook herself and walked over to her side.

Emily sighed and then started pulling dishes out of the rack and putting them away, trying not to think about Dev and Landon. About the fact that Dev had asked her to come over, had said he wanted to be with her.

That couldn't happen.

She needed to back off and create a distance, but it was getting harder and harder to make herself do that.

Emily's shocked "no" still rang in Dev's ears the next day as he swept the floor outside the library, cleaning up a mess of popcorn someone had spilled.

And why wouldn't she have sounded shocked? For one thing, she didn't think of Dev that way, he was pretty sure. For another, she must have thought he was asking for more than just her company.

He hadn't been…had he? He'd just spoken from his heart; he hadn't wanted the evening, their connection and warmth and new openness, to come to an end.

It was all for the best, though. He couldn't have someone like Emily, and he shouldn't be getting so close to her.

"Dev?" He turned, and she was there. Behind her in the library, a small group of students labored over notebooks. "About last night. I'm sorry. I didn't mean to push you out. I just… I'm not up for…whatever it was you were looking for."

He leaned his broom against the cleaning cart and wiped his hands with a clean towel. "I'm the one who should apologize. When I asked you to come over, I was out of line. I didn't mean… you know. I wouldn't ask that. I was just enjoying being with you, and I didn't want it to stop."

It was all true. He wouldn't ask anything inappropriate of her, but he did long for her company.

She was staring at the ground, face red.

"I can keep more of a distance," he said. "I don't want to push, but I felt for you last night, for what you told me. If you need a friend, I'm here."

She raised her head slowly and met his eyes,

and Dev seemed to see a spark, bright and dazzling, arc between them.

"Thanks," she said. "I could use a friend."

"Me, too." He felt like something more needed to be said. "And in the spirit of being a friend, I won't try anything. No touching, no nothing."

Her cheeks flushed pink. "Okay."

"So, friends?" He held out a hand.

"Friends."

And he could control the part of his heart that wanted more than friendship from Emily Carver.

After that awkward conversation, things got easier between them. They fell into friend-like patterns, eating meals together, hanging out with Landon together, talking about things. It was good. It was friendly.

And if it made Dev want more, want what he couldn't have, well, so be it. He could handle it.

Chapter Nine

Normally, Emily loved going to the Miners' Diner. The homey atmosphere and real local food were just right, and it was right for her budget, too.

And normally, she loved going out to eat with her best friend. Hayley was fun and funny and wise, and even if Emily had had a bad day at work, Hayley usually joked her into a better mood.

Today, though, Hayley had a gleam in her eye that told Emily something was going on. And when Hayley asked for a table in the back corner, she got even more curious. What was on Hayley's mind?

They walked past Doc Harper, who was still the county's main physician at seventy-two. He was having dinner with his younger brother, the area's premier veterinarian, a young-looking, vital seventy-year-old.

Jennie, a longtime waitress, came over as soon as they'd sat down at the directed table. "Good to see you ladies. How's life up at the school? Can I bring you drinks? Or a Cinco de Mayo appetizer?"

"Iced tea for me, thanks," Hayley said.

"Just water." Economizing was one of Emily's superpowers. Someone had once told her how much money the average person spent on beverages in a year, and she'd decided on the spot to never order anything but water at a restaurant again.

Then again, she had a little extra money now. She could afford to treat her friend. "We'll celebrate Cinco de Mayo with an order of nachos to share while we look at the menu."

"Coming right up."

As soon as Jennie was out of earshot, Hayley put down her menu and leaned forward. "So tell me everything."

"About what?"

"You and Dev!"

"What about us?" Emily studied her menu for another minute before looking up at her friend.

Hayley pulled it out of her hands. "You're together every day! Stan says you eat dinner at each other's places almost every night."

Emily could have strangled Stan and his nosy

ways. "Not *every* night. It's just… Sometimes it's easier, since we're together for Landon's tutoring after school. And we're friends."

"*Close* friends?" Hayley waggled her eyebrows.

Emily sighed. Clearly, Hayley wasn't going to take the hint that Emily didn't want to talk about it. "No. Not close. We, well, we agreed to be just friends."

Hayley stared. "It was *discussed*?"

"Uh-huh. And that's what we agreed."

The nachos arrived, and Jennie took their order and stuck around for a minute to share the local gossip. Then the Harper brothers came over to say hello and discuss a fundraiser they were helping with at the school. Lady bucked her training and jumped up to put her front paws onto her vet's lap, earning an ear rub instead of a scolding. Country music played on the old-fashioned jukebox. By the time the men had headed out, Emily's trout and Hayley's elk burger had arrived, and they dug in.

"Mmm, there's nothing like the Miners' Diner," Hayley said. "I'm not going to eat again for a week."

Emily laughed. "I'm taking the rest of these nachos to Dev and Landon. There's no way we can…" She trailed off, seeing Hayley's expression.

"See? See that? You're talking about them like they're your family. There's more than a convenient friendship going on here." She held up a hand. "Which is fine! Totally fine. I'm happy for you. You deserve to settle down and be happy."

"It's not like that. It isn't." Emily looked down at her plate, but her appetite was suddenly gone. "We're friends, and that's all, and that's that."

Hayley tilted her head to one side. "Still punishing yourself, are you?"

"Not sure what you mean." She so did not want to go into this, but she knew Hayley. The woman was relentless and wouldn't give up until she'd wrung every secret out of Emily. It would have made Emily mad, except that she knew Hayley cared and had her best interests at heart.

"Well, for example," Hayley said, "you organize that 5-K race in memory of Mitch, because his parents want you to, even though it's a miserable experience and doesn't even raise much money."

"Don't remind me," Emily groaned. "I'm expecting a call from them any day now. We said last year was the final one, but I just know they'll want to keep it going."

"Yeah, as long as you do all the work. If they call, you should say you won't do it."

"Well..." The thought was undeniably tempting, but it also made her stomach churn with anxiety.

"You're always looking for ways to deny yourself happiness to make up for your so-called mistakes," Hayley said. "Isn't it time to stop? Give yourself a break and look for some happiness?"

"I'm happy," Emily said. "Pretty happy. And being around Dev and Landon is nice. Fun." She looked through her lashes to see if Hayley was buying it.

"Nope. I've seen how you look at each other, and it doesn't spell fun. It spells wanting and caring and romance."

"It does not— Wait. Does he look at *me* that way?"

Hayley made her thumb and forefinger into a gun shape and pointed it at Emily. "Bang, you've got it. He does. But why would you care, if all you want is to be friends?"

Emily stuffed down the happiness that wanted to rise in her at the thought of Dev looking at her in some kind of special way.

It didn't matter. Maybe he had a lack of prospects so far here in Little Mesa, but that wouldn't last. He was too good, too kind, too attractive to stay single for long.

And even if he *did* have more than a passing interest in Emily, she wasn't going to let him act on it. There was a reason she had lived through the fire when she wanted to die, and it wasn't to enjoy herself. It was to help others. To teach.

Not to be a wife and mother. She'd already had her chance at that, and she'd failed.

"What's going through your head right now?" Hayley asked.

Emily shrugged. "Just the fact that I'm not going to be anything more than friends with Dev or anyone. Reminding myself of that."

"Because you're a horrible human being who doesn't deserve happiness?" Haley raised an eyebrow and took another bite of her burger.

"Well…it sounds stupid when you say it like that, but yes."

Hayley gestured with her burger, swallowed her bite and glared. "It *sounds* stupid because it *is* stupid! Do you know how many Christians the apostle Paul persecuted before his conversion? And yet he was forgiven and went on to evangelize the world and practically write the New Testament!"

Emily fought back a smile at her friend's dramatic version of the story. "He didn't get married, though."

"That's debatable, and anyway, how did we get on the apostle Paul? We're talking about you and your ridiculous plan to deny yourself happiness because you think you were at fault in the deaths of your family. But tragic as that whole thing was, I don't think anyone but you would lay all the blame about that at your feet. What about your husband? What about your mom?"

Emily leaned back and slid down a little on the booth's bench. She looked up at the rough-hewn rafters, wagon wheels hanging down from them, wired with lights. "We've gone over all this before. Mom wasn't able to think straight—"

"But you didn't *know* that," Hayley interrupted. "Her dementia wasn't diagnosed."

"I was her daughter. I should have seen it. And I for sure knew Mitch had a drinking problem. I was the competent adult. The *only* competent adult, as it turned out, and I failed."

"We all fail at things!" Hayley sounded positively fierce. "Do you think I've never done anything wrong in my life, never made any mistakes?"

That startled Emily. "Yeah, I do think that," she admitted. "Nothing serious, anyway."

"Well, you're wrong. And yet here I am, putting myself out there, embracing life. Because that's what God wants us to do."

Emily studied her friend, eyes narrowed. "I want to hear about these mistakes in your past."

"That's for another time. We're talking about you. How you need to let Dev and Landon in."

Emily opened her mouth to make another reasonable, logical argument, but her feelings rebelled. Why was Hayley pushing her like this rather than being her usual supportive self? "Don't you think I want to let them in? Do you think it's easy to keep them at a distance? You have no idea how much I want to give Landon all the hugs he needs and, and explore things with Dev, but I can't. I can't. Do you understand that?"

Hayley shook her head. "No, I really don't."

"Then don't criticize what you don't understand."

Hayley bit her lip and looked off to the side, toward the now-crowded restaurant. But it was obvious she wasn't seeing the people there.

After a minute, she looked back at Emily, leaned forward and gripped her hands. "I'm only going to say this once," she said. "You're making a huge mistake, and you're fooling yourself if you think it's going to work out for you to keep all your feelings squashed down. Not to mention that you're insulting God."

"Insulting *God*?"

"That's what I said. Because God has the power to do anything. Any. Thing. That's what Scripture tells us. If you don't believe Jesus can wash you clean, are you really even a Christian?"

"Hayley!" Emily slid out of the booth and stood, snapping her fingers for Lady to come to attention. "I love you, my friend, but I'm not going to sit here and let you question my faith. Come on, or I'll find another ride home."

Inside, she was reeling. Hayley had thrown her for a loop. Was her best friend right, that she was insulting God by not accepting His forgiveness?

But God knew her inside and out, and He knew that every time she got close to a date, or a man, or any kind of happiness, she locked up inside. She had to assume He was making that happen because she didn't deserve to have whatever was on offer.

Their ride back to school was quiet. Emily expected Hayley to apologize, or take back what she'd said, but she didn't. She just pulled up to Emily's cabin and stopped.

"Thanks for the ride," Emily said stiffly. "Come on, Lady."

The shaggy poodle mix jumped out of Hayley's back seat and trotted into the little yard.

"Guess I'll see you later," Emily said.

"Think about what I said," Hayley said. "Think about what you're missing. You could have things the rest of us only dream about. Don't throw them away."

She wasn't throwing them away, Emily thought

as she let herself into the cabin. She was seeing them on the other side of a fine sheet of gauze, but they simply weren't accessible to her.

On Friday, Dev was headed back to his cabin when Stan flagged him down. "Need your help with something," the white-haired math teacher said.

"Sure." Dev was bone tired, but Stan was a neighbor.

Stan led him over to the side of his cabin and indicated a square of ground that was marked off with stakes and twine. "I need to dig this up and work in some compost," he said. "Hoping you'll help. I got an extra shovel."

Dev blew out a breath. Maybe the teacher had been sitting at a desk all day, but Dev had been lifting and hauling, doing physical work. The last thing he wanted was more of that.

But Landon was over at the boys' cabins, having a supervised playdate—only Dev wasn't allowed to call it that, of course, because Landon was *way* too old—with a couple of the other boys. Dev had no plans, and he'd already learned that Friday nights could be lonely up here in the mountains with little else than the stars for company.

A hawk swung its solitary way across the sky as the sun sank toward the mountains, lighting them up with a rose-gold glow. Around him, in the trees beside the cabin, chickadees fluttered and dived, calling out cheery greetings to one another. Sage and pine scents blew in on a cool breeze.

Even though Dev had done physical work all day, he'd been stuck inside. "Sure, I'll help." He took the shovel Stan offered and started digging. "Planning a vegetable garden, are you?"

"Sure am. It's tough up here, a short growing season, but working with the earth keeps me sane." Stan grinned. "Plus, the new horticulture therapist is a real beauty. I'll consult with her."

So I'm digging your garden to help your love life?

The work wasn't easy. The ground was dry and hard. And it seemed to Dev that he was digging at twice the pace that Stan was. Oh, well. The guy was probably twenty years older than Dev. Dev was grateful he had the health to work hard.

He doubled down to it, figuring he'd get the job done as soon as possible and then head home to a shower and the hockey game.

"Noticed you've been spending quite a bit of time with Emily," Stan said out of nowhere, leaning on his shovel.

Dev's senses went on alert. He kept shoveling but studied the white-haired man from the corner of his eye. "Yeah?"

"We're a little protective of our own," Stan said. "We—or I, rather, I shouldn't speak for anyone else—I'm a little concerned."

The *we* and *our own* language made Dev feel like the outsider, but he supposed that was only right: he *was* the newcomer and the outsider. And Stan had the right to be protective. "It's just fallen out that way since she's tutoring Landon," he explained. "We're friends, or getting to be. That's all."

"Uh-huh." Stan started digging again, not responding further, as if waiting for Dev to go on.

But there was nothing more to say. He wasn't the type of man a smart, educated woman like Emily would go for. He'd known that, but she'd made it even clearer last week when she'd backed off his invitation to continue their conversation at his place.

Rubbing the tension from her shoulders had felt wonderful. But it wouldn't happen again. He'd given his word that he wouldn't touch her, and he didn't go back on his word.

"She's been through a lot, you know. Had a hard time." Stan was digging steadily now.

"I gathered that, from her burns."

"Right. And I'm pretty sure there's more to that fire story."

Dev frowned. "More than what?"

"Pretty sure she lost more than her looks."

Dev stared at the man. "She didn't lose her looks. She has some scars, that's all."

"Uh-huh." Stan's eyes were steady on him. "Ask her about it sometime. If you're her *friend*."

He was curious enough that he would. But Stan's words rang another bell. "Are you telling me to stay away because you're interested in her yourself?" Stan was way too old, but to some guys, that didn't matter. Stan seemed to like younger ladies.

"Me? No. Not my type."

"Uh-huh." Dev thrust his shovel into the hard soil, irritated for reasons he didn't fully understand.

"But if you're not serious about her, then you *should* stay away," Stan said, his voice gruff. "She's a good gal."

"I'm not serious about her. She's not for me."

It was true; she wasn't. She was way too smart for him. Way too professionally advanced.

"Good. I think that's best."

Stan's words were nothing more than what Dev had thought himself, but he still didn't like hearing them from the older man. "I can finish this myself," Dev said, waving his hand at the half-dug garden. He'd do it all if he could get this irritating man out of his way.

Not paying attention to whether Stan stayed or left, Dev went back to digging the garden, hard.

He was angry about all of it. Angry that he couldn't learn and that his lack of intelligence ruled out a woman of the sort he actually liked. A woman like Emily.

Why hadn't God given him a good brain?

But Landon would have the advantages and would improve his ability to learn. That was the important thing.

He kept digging, trying to lose himself in the work, to shut out thoughts of what he couldn't have.

Landon's future and happiness were a lot more important than the ache in Dev's heart.

Chapter Ten

Emily walked into the church building the next Sunday, steeled for the pain she knew the day would bring.

At least, she *thought* she was steeled for it. But when she saw Hayley passing out carnations to all the grandmothers and mothers, saw everyone cooing over several new babies, she nearly turned around and walked out.

Mother's Day. For many women, a highlight of the year. But when you'd lost a child and were losing your mother a little at a time to an awful disease, every Mother's Day was painful. She'd had two beautiful, happy Mother's Days and six excruciating ones after that.

Hayley handed her a carnation, her eyes full of sympathy. "These are for all women, of course. We all find ways to nurture others. But you'd be forgiven for staying home today, you know. Watching a service on TV or just reading your Bible and worshipping on your own."

"No, I'm fine." She wasn't, but she hadn't come to church so people would feel sorry for her.

"You sure do love to beat yourself up." Hayley hugged her. "If you want to get together after, I'm here. And…listen, I'm sorry I was intrusive at the diner. You have to make your own choices and live your own life."

"It's fine. I know you were saying it all out of care. And thanks for the offer, but I'm going to see Mom later today." She didn't want to fuel Hayley's concerns by admitting that her car wasn't fixed yet and that Dev was taking her.

The sun shone through the little sanctuary's stained glass windows, and the organ music played softly, not muffling people's excited conversations. The kids were doing a special music performance today, it seemed.

Landon wouldn't be in the performance, since he was spending the weekend in Denver visiting his mom.

But she thought of him. Thought of how tall he was, and how her own child might have been that tall.

Would James have resembled her side of the family more, or Mitch's? Would he have liked to read?

Would he have made her something special for Mother's Day, or would he consider himself too grown-up for such emotional stuff?

Automatically, she reached for Lady, but the dog wasn't there. Why had she left Lady at home today? Without the comfort and support of her service dog, Emily just might fall apart.

Maybe Hayley was right. Maybe Emily was obsessed with punishing herself.

She tried to control the tears, but they were dripping down. Tried to remind herself that other women suffered, too: some had lost a baby to miscarriage or a child to cancer, others had lost their own mothers, and some were estranged from mother or child. She'd even participated in a focus group the pastor had conducted, as he'd honed his ideas about how to frame the Mother's Day service so it was sensitive to the various ways Mother's Day could cause pain.

She felt for other women, but their circumstances didn't take away her own pain. She dug in her purse for a tissue and wiped her eyes. When she took a deep breath and looked around the congregation, she saw several people looking at her, concerned or curious expressions on their faces.

This might not work, sitting through church. In previous years, she'd avoided it.

This year she'd decided to try, but she might not be able to do it. And if she was going to be an emotional mess, she'd bring others down, others who were even now oohing and aahing as the little children came in to sing a special song.

She watched as the children finished their song and ran to their mothers, seated in the congregation. As women picked up their beautiful, healthy children, sat them on their laps, praised them, Emily felt as jealous as a child at a birthday party, watching the birthday girl get a pony.

Which was wrong and mean and ridiculous. She should be happy for all those women. Should remember that, however sweet everything looked on Mother's Day at church, they all could be struggling—to support their children, to handle a difficult relationship with the father, to deal with a child's illness or behavior problems.

But it didn't help. She'd have welcomed those motherly struggles compared to the sheer emptiness and hollowness she felt now.

She wiped her face as best she could, looking around at the banners on the church wall. One caught her eye, bright green lettering on a white background. "And be ye kind one to another, tenderhearted, forgiving one another, even as God for Christ's sake hath forgiven you."

Had she forgiven her mother, and Mitch, for their part in the fire and the loss of lives therein?

And then the second part of the verse seemed to blink at her like a neon sign: *even as God for Christ's sake hath forgiven you.*

God had forgiven her.

Had He, though? Had He really?

She clutched her carnation and watched the little children file out. Prayed along with the pastor and his sensitive thoughtful prayer.

Tried to tell herself, over and over, that she could do this, had to do this, had to learn to live in the world with all its celebrations and holidays. If it hurt, she deserved it.

At least, she'd always thought she deserved it, but was Hayley right? Was she flagellating herself, throwing away God's gift of forgiveness?

When the congregation stood to sing the opening hymn, the pain grew too sharp. She slipped out, weaving apologetically past the family that had filled in her pew, keeping her head down to avoid showing her makeup-streaked, wet-with-tears face.

She'd tried, she really had. But she couldn't do it. So she'd go home and wrap Mom's gift.

She'd pretend to sleep on the way to the care home, maybe. That way, she wouldn't have to make happy conversation with the man she was developing way too many feelings for but couldn't have.

At seven thirty that evening, on the way home from driving Emily to visit her mother, Dev slowed his truck on the mountain road, squinting.

Emily had been dozing. "What's going on?" she asked sleepily.

He liked her sleepy voice, a little too much, so he focused on the road. "There it is." He saw a small sign, then a pull-off.

She sat up straighter, reaching back to touch Lady in the back seat, as Dev pulled the truck over a rutted parking area and stopped.

Sure enough, there was a bench. And an amazing vista before them.

The setting sun emerged from behind a purple cloud, shining golden onto the closer foothills, making them glow. More distant were the dark peaks behind which the sun would settle in just a short time.

He'd really, really wanted to help Emily feel better ever since he'd seen her so broken up in church. He assumed it was because of her mom being sick, which had to make Mother's Day difficult. And indeed, she'd had a rough visit today.

Dev had gone into the care home with her for half an hour, but he'd soon discerned that his presence wasn't helping to calm the older woman, was maybe making her worse. So he'd gone out to wait in the truck. He'd sat there using the phone app he'd recently found, a learn-to-read app for adults. He was working on decoding and comprehension, and it wasn't awful, especially if he took breaks every twenty minutes or so. He felt like a dork working on such simple stuff, but he found himself really wanting to improve his skills. Maybe, just maybe, if he could make enough progress, he'd keep up with his son and feel more on a level with Emily.

Finally, she'd come out of the care home, her face pale and drawn. But when he'd asked her about it, she'd shrugged. "Mom's Mom, and she wasn't having a great day. At least they're not hassling me about paying my bill now. I have you to thank for that."

He was floored by her ability to focus on the positive. He was also starving, they both were, so they'd stopped at a taco truck and grabbed a couple of tacos each. Conscious of Stan's protective warnings about Emily, he'd kept it light, not a sit-down restaurant where things could be romantic, but a quick stop for tacos.

Only she'd gotten into a conversation with the family operating the food truck, and he'd joined in. They'd sat down at the picnic table outside the truck to eat and ended up talking to two of the kids in the family. They both liked kids and spoke Spanish, so it had turned into a fun experience.

In certain ways, he and Emily were really compatible.

But at the end of the impromptu visit, the little girl had hugged her mother and talked about Mother's Day, and they'd argued about the date, which was different in Mexico than in the US this year. And Emily had gotten sad again.

Now, she climbed out of the truck at his urging, but her movements were mechanical. Clearly, she wasn't her usual upbeat self.

And then she saw the view and her face lit up. She had a really, really pretty smile, and when she smiled, her cheeks flushed a little under that fair white skin. Like a pink rose just blooming, and when did he ever get poetic? But she inspired him.

He came around to her side of the truck. "Let's sit for a few," he said. "Landon won't be home until late tonight, so I'm not in a big hurry. Are you?"

She shook her head. "No. Not since Lady's here with us. Come on, girl."

The big dog jumped out of the truck and started sniffing.

They walked over and sat down on the bench, Lady on a long lead and sniffing around the area.

"How'd you find this place?" she asked as she looked around. "I've lived around here for a long time, but I never knew there was such a cool viewing spot here."

"Stan told me about it, actually."

"I didn't know you and Stan were getting to be friends."

He held out a flat hand, tilted it from side to side. "Kinda. More like he's taken it on himself to give me advice."

"Yeah? Like what?" She sounded amused. "He's a big-time mansplainer, but I didn't know he'd do it to another man."

Should he tell her? But they seemed alone in the world, alone except for the dog and the little vole she was chasing after, and the eagle soaring overhead. It made him want to be as open as the landscape before them, and while he couldn't do that, he could at least share some of what Stan had said. "For one thing, he told me to stay away from you."

"What?" She jerked around to face him, staring. "What do you mean?"

Dev lifted his hands, palms up. "He noticed we were spending a lot of time together. Let me know it wasn't a good idea."

Her eyes narrowed. "Since when does he have a say over how I spend my time? Or how you do?"

He shrugged. "I explained that we were just friends, but he didn't believe it."

She stared at him for a moment longer, then looked out toward the distant mountain range. The anger seemed to seep out of her. "Yeah. Hayley noticed, too."

He wanted to know whether Hayley had warned her off him, but he was too afraid of the answer to ask. "People keep matching us up because we spend so much time together," he said instead. "But we're neighbors, and you're tutoring Landon. Can't a man and a woman be friends?"

"Right?" She looked back at him.

Once their gazes tangled, he couldn't look away. Her eyes darkened as he looked at her, and his heart rate sped up.

Which pretty much negated his point. "I'm not going to say it's easy," he said slowly.

Her forehead creased, and she bit her lip.

"Don't worry," he said. He wanted to reach for her, put a reassuring hand on her shoulder. Holding back almost killed him, but he did it. "I made you a promise not to touch you. I'll stick to that."

She nodded quickly, looked away off over the mountains.

The sun was sinking behind them, sending out light-filled rays, tinting the sky pink and gold. "Wow," she said softly.

"Yeah." The need to pull her close was palpable, a living thing.

A bird swooped past them and to the ground, then back up. Gray wings, brown-and-black-patterned back. A gray head with black-and-white cheeks. Lady went alert, watching it.

"It's a kestrel!" Emily exclaimed.

"Sparrow hawk!" he said at the same time.

They both laughed. "I think it's the same thing," he said, relieved—kind of—that the romantic moment had passed.

"Really?" She pulled out her phone, tapped something into it. "You're right. Look." She held out her phone, and the sudden movement made the small hawk fly up, calling *Klee! Klee!* Lady barked sharply, straining at the leash Emily had tightened.

Dev didn't expect the creature to come back, but it did, flying down, then up again.

"That's a mating ritual," she said, reading from her phone. "There must be a female nearby. That's so cool!"

He loved her ability to get excited about

things, to forget her problems. It made her fun to be with.

They sat for a little while then, watching the sunset. The breeze got cool and she shivered a minute, then scooted over close. "It's silly to stick to a rule for a rule's sake," she said. "It's cold, but so pretty. I don't want to leave just yet. And friends are allowed to keep each other warm, right?"

He found an extra jacket in his truck and wrapped it around her, but she still snuggled close and rested her head on his arm. "You know, Mother's Day is hard for me for a particular reason," she said. "I really appreciate your company."

"Want to talk about it?"

"I'm just going to tell you quick. I don't want to dig into all the feelings." She sucked in a breath. "Okay. That fire, where Mom and I got burned? I... I lost my husband. And my two-year-old son."

All the breath whooshed out of him, and he pulled her close and wrapped his arms around her, because a hug was the only way to react to such horror. "That's... I don't even know what to say."

"That's just it. There's nothing to say." Her voice sounded a little ragged. "Not gonna pretend I'm fine now, but I'm functioning. I just wanted you to know, but I don't really want to talk about it."

He cuddled her close then, head spinning as his view of her broke and resettled. He'd known she had experienced trouble in her life, but he hadn't had an inkling of how bad it had been. She'd had awful problems, and for all that, she kept making her way through.

Admiration for her surged, and with it, tender compassion. "I'm so sorry," he said.

"Thanks." She turned her face up to look at him. "Friends help. And…and Landon helps. Sometimes being around him is hard, because James would have been just Landon's age. But I think he's helping me heal."

"Just Landon's… Oh, wow." He touched her cheek, wanting to show his sympathy.

"Thanks," she said. "But Landon's a great kid. I think it's healing me to know him, and to see that life goes on."

A strand of hair blew across her face, and he brushed it back, and another emotion blended smoothly in with the sympathy he felt for her. "You're something else, you know?"

She met his eyes for a moment and then looked away, her cheeks going pink. "I'm not. I've made so many mistakes. You have no idea."

"Maybe not," he said, "but I can see your

heart." Emotions surged in him, mixed, con-flicting, intense.

And then, because he wanted to blot away the pain in her eyes, and because he was only human, he lowered his head and pressed his lips to hers.

Chapter Eleven

Dev's kiss felt perfect. Gentle and respectful, but not hesitant. He wanted to kiss her, *really* wanted to kiss her, and he let her know that with energy.

Emily relaxed into his arms, warmth spreading through her. How long had it been since someone had held her? She was used to being the caretaker, the teacher, the one responsible. She'd stopped thinking someone might take care of her, but that was what Dev's embrace felt like, and she loved it.

Lady settled at their feet with a gusty sigh.

He cupped her face as he kissed her, treating her as if she were precious and fragile. His hands were rough with work, yet so gentle as he brushed one over her hair and let his finger trace her jawline.

The kiss, the embrace, felt so new and so

special that it chased rational thought from her mind. She hadn't been kissed for a long time, and she tried to remember the reason for it. There was a reason for it. She wasn't supposed to be kissing Dev.

But she couldn't think—she could only feel. His touch, so tender, swept her worries straight out of her mind.

He lifted his lips from hers and looked at her, his brown eyes warm. "Is this okay?"

In some part of her mind she knew that the answer was *no*. It wasn't okay, but instead of focusing on that, she let her own fingers tangle in his hair. Springy, short, coarser than hers.

She felt so good being close to Dev like this. He was so tender, so caring. So much what she didn't deserve.

But she didn't want to think about that. Instead, she turned her head and rested her cheek against his chest and let him hold her, felt the breeze on her face, opened her eyes to drink in the beauty of their surroundings. He had brought her here. He had cared enough to want to show her this special place, to make her feel better, and it was good of him. *He* was good.

And then all the old feelings forced their way back into her heart. He might be good, but she wasn't. She wasn't supposed to feel this good, wasn't allowed to, wouldn't let herself. The small worries built up steam until she tugged away.

He let her go, but only after the slightest tightening of his hands told her he didn't want to let her go.

She didn't deserve a man who didn't want to let her go. The moment she left his arms, the rest of the old, bad feelings rushed back in.

She didn't deserve any of this.

She stood, and it felt like tearing herself away from the best thing that had ever happened to her, but she had to do it. "I have to go. We have to go. Right away."

He stood and shook his head the way Lady shook off water. "Wait. Can you slow down? Just a little?"

His voice magnetized her, and she knew if she didn't break away now, she wouldn't be able to, and that would be wrong. "No, I can't slow down," she said. "Let's go."

She walked over to the truck and gripped the cold door handle. Cold. Hard. That was what she needed to focus on. Not beautiful, tender warmth.

"Emily?" He came to stand behind her, very close. "Are you okay?"

She stared at that cold, hard silver door handle and shook her head.

"Can we talk about it?"

Again, she shook her head without looking at him.

The ride back to the school was quiet. Twice, Dev tried to open a conversation, but Emily didn't respond.

She was churning inside. Why had she let him kiss her? Why had she practically initiated it herself? Why had he gone along, after he promised not to touch her?

She knew it wasn't fair to blame him, knew the kiss had been mutual, but she had to find a way to push away this appealing, magnetic man, this man who was much too good for her.

So when he pulled up into the driveway, she got out and paced back and forth. "Dev, that can't happen again. I don't want it."

"I'm sorry, Emily," he said. "I thought... Never mind."

Lady was nudging at her, clearly sensing Emily's agitation. In fact, her heart was pounding; she was on the verge of a panic attack. How had she... Why had she... "I have to go inside," she said.

"Emily, wait," Dev said. He picked up something inside the truck and handed it to her, her bag. The bag that had held her Mother's Day present—the gift that she'd taken to her mother, who hadn't known what it was and had pushed it away.

Dealing with her mother was a trial, and it grieved her every time she went. These last two weeks, when Dev had taken her, she'd looked forward to it, but not because of Mom. Because she got to spend time with Dev—Dev and sometimes Landon.

She'd let herself get attached to them. Let expectations and hopes build that shouldn't have been there.

"Look, I'll keep teaching Landon, but I need to stay away from you. That was unacceptable." She hated the harsh words coming out of her mouth, but it was the only way she could do what was right.

Dev's expression hardened. He opened his mouth as if to say something and then shut it again and studied her. "I see," he said finally, and she could read the hurt in his eyes.

No, you don't see, she wanted to scream at him. She wanted to pull him back into her arms, to explain that it wasn't something about him, that it was about her. She wasn't good enough for him.

But none of that would make sense to him. Better to hurt him a little now than a lot later.

So she spun on her heel, snapped her fingers for Lady to follow and marched into her cold, lonely cabin.

* * *

By the end of the school day on Monday, Dev was beat. He hadn't slept well after that disastrous kiss with Emily. And then he'd stressed out all day trying, and failing, to avoid her. There was a broken window in the library he had to fix. He'd passed her in the hall three times. And though he'd gone to the staff lunchroom at a different time than either of them usually did, she'd been there. Probably trying to avoid him the same way he was trying to avoid her.

Never had the Bright Tomorrows school seemed so small.

When Landon rushed out the doors of the school and ran to him, practically bursting with excitement, Dev immediately felt better. Back in Denver, and in the early days here, Landon had trudged out of school with a frown on his face. In just five weeks, Landon's attitude toward his classes had undergone a complete turnaround. He wasn't making As, but he was passing, keeping up. That was worth any amount of embarrassment on Dev's part.

"Dad! Can I join the drama club? Will you help build the set? I already said you would."

"Drama club?" Dev smiled to see his son's excitement.

"Yeah! They do a performance at the end of the year, and they need more people, and they're doing a play about superheroes! Not the exact same ones as in movies, 'cause of copy, copy something—"

"Copyright?" They walked slowly down the lane toward the cabin, the sounds of shouting, glad-to-be-done-with-school boys diminishing behind them. The sun shone down on them, warm like summer. The snow-capped mountains in the distance seemed far away.

"Yeah! And I can be, like, one of the helper heroes, if I can remember lines. Or maybe someone who gets hurt, and then I could have fake blood all over me!"

Not for the first time, Dev was impressed with Bright Tomorrows and the way the school engaged the boys. He'd never have expected a school for troubled boys to have an enthusiastic drama club, but if they put on superhero plays, it made sense. "Wait, how come they're only starting the spring play now?" School here went on longer than ordinary schools, well into June, but classes would end in just six weeks.

"They do a lot of plays and they're starting a new one, and I have to decide this week." Finally, Landon was running out of breath. "Sometimes they don't have a fancy set, but if you help, they could, and all the guys want you to."

"It sounds pretty good." Dev was learning

not to say yes right away, though. "Let's think it through." They were approaching their cabin now, and from the other direction, Emily was approaching hers.

Dev's stomach plunged. She'd taken the long way around. Trying to avoid him, most likely.

For the thousandth time, he kicked himself mentally for kissing her. Why hadn't he stuck to his no-touching plan?

But he knew why. When he'd seen Emily's willingness to be close, when he'd felt her snuggling against him in the cool mountain air, all his willpower had blown away on the breeze. He'd given in, and for a few blissful minutes, he'd gotten lost in her sweet perfume and soft hair and tender, hesitant touch.

And then it had all gone wrong. He didn't quite understand why she'd abruptly backed away and cooled off and gotten angry, but it had happened and now he had to deal with the fallout.

He dearly wished they weren't neighbors. He wished she wasn't Landon's tutor. But wishes weren't reality.

"Please, Dad? I really want to."

Thinking about Emily, and tutoring, reminded him of the major obstacle to Landon joining the drama club. "You have tutoring after school."

"Yeah, but... Hey, Ms. Carver! Ms. Carver!" Landon waved frantically and then ran ahead to meet Emily. "You gotta talk to Dad about the drama club!"

She smiled—obviously fake and forced—and let Landon grab her hand and tug her toward Dev. They met on the road in front of their two cabins.

Dev couldn't force a smile. "Sorry," he said to her. "Landon's excited."

"I can see." She ran an affectionate hand over Landon's hair. "We do need to talk about the drama club."

"Tutoring is the most important thing," Dev said.

"Oh, Dad..."

"You have to pass the achievement tests at the end of the year to go on to fourth grade. That's what we need to focus on." He looked at Emily, forced himself to see her as a professional, not as the soft, warm woman he'd held in his arms. "Is there a way to do both? Would that be a good idea, or too much?"

"It's great Landon wants to participate. I think we can make it work." She stroked Landon's hair again, and Landon leaned against her, and Dev's heart gave a big, painful thump as worry filled his mind.

Landon was getting attached to Emily, and from the looks of things, it went both ways.

Emily was a good person, the type of person he'd want Landon to attach to. Even, if God willed it, the type of person who'd make a good stepmother to Landon.

And a good wife to Dev, except that she didn't want to be anywhere near him. In fact, maybe she was trying to get out of tutoring Landon as a way to avoid Dev. "I still need for you to tutor him," he reminded her. He wished, now, that they'd done a formal contract. "We can make... adjustments, about where it happens. Do it right after school in the library, and I can pick him up afterward."

She glanced quickly at him and then away, but it was enough for him to see that she understood: he was offering to make it so she didn't have to spend time with him. He wasn't going to force himself on her.

"Drama club's right after school," Landon protested.

"Every day?"

"Three days a week," Emily said. "And I can guarantee that after rehearsal, Landon isn't going to be up for tutoring. We might have to work together in the mornings on those days, before school."

A picture flashed before Dev's eyes: Emily

in the morning, sleepy, hair mussed, drinking coffee at the same breakfast table as him and Landon. Longing rose up in him, but he pushed it away, forced himself to be a neutral, concerned parent. "As his tutor, what do you think? Would it be a good idea to change his routine like this?"

Landon looked up at her, his eyes wide. "It would be, Ms. Carver! I'd still do all my schoolwork!"

"You don't like getting up early," Dev reminded him.

"I can do it! I can set my own alarm."

Emily smiled at Landon and then looked at Dev with a bland, professional expression. "It's good Landon is so motivated," she said. "It would be good for his confidence and his reading skills."

"And you're willing to change the schedule?"

"Of course. In fact, I'd need to change it anyway, because—"

"Yay! And you'll help with the sets, right?" Landon bounced up and down, his smile wide and confident, like he knew Dev would do it.

And Dev was a sucker. He wanted Landon to be that certain of his father's willingness to help. "Okay. As long as you keep improving in school, you can do it, and I'll help."

"I asked Dad if he could build the sets for us,"

Landon explained to Emily, holding her hand and swinging on it.

"That's...great," she said without enthusiasm.

Her tone was strange, and he wondered why.

And then he knew. "Who's running the drama club?" he asked.

"Three of us take turns," she said. "And it's my turn."

Their gazes held for the shortest moment as Dev processed just what he'd agreed to.

Instead of spending less time together, they'd be spending more.

Chapter Twelve

The school stage was a part of the multipurpose hall that served as the gymnasium, the cafeteria and the assembly room. As such, it always smelled slightly of kids' sneakers and whatever Hayley had served up for lunch. The good news was that the mostly glass wall that looked out to the mountains could be opened to allow the kids to roll tables outside in good weather.

Plus, importantly, it let in fresh air. So Emily pushed it wide-open before she gathered the student actors and stagehands at the long table closest to the stage. To avoid distracting the kids, she'd already taken Lady to a sunny corner of the cafeteria and given her the "stay" command.

"Do we have to memorize a lot of lines?" Chip Peterson, so nicknamed for his love of potato chips, held a bag of his favorite snack.

"I want to be in the play, but I'm no good at remembering stuff."

"Memorizing is part of it, but we'll have prompters just like people on TV do." That was thanks to a grant from one of the school's generous benefactors.

A shadow crossed Landon's face, and Emily was pretty sure she knew why. A teleprompter only worked if you knew how to read. Landon, like some of the other kids who were eager to be involved, wasn't a strong reader. His lessons were helping, and he was improving, but he had miles to go before he could glance at a teleprompter, read what was on it and carry on acting without the audience noticing the extra support.

The flip side of that was that kids who didn't read well were often good memorizers. "Part of what I'll be doing over the next few days is talking through the parts with all of you, figuring out your strengths. We'll make sure that everyone gets a part he likes and that he can succeed at." It was a tall promise, but one Emily felt confident making. She'd chosen the play because of its appeal to young boys and its balanced mixture of parts in a true ensemble cast.

The boys were talking among themselves now, passing around snacks, speculating about what parts they might get but also telling stories about their days and tossing paper wads and shoving and elbowing each other, getting physical. Emily knew she had to put them to work soon or she'd lose them. "One last thing, and I want everyone to listen up," she said and waited until she had their attention. "Being in this play can't take away from your schoolwork. If you have homework to do or a meeting with a teacher, you let me know and we'll work out a way for you to do it while staying in the play. Got it?"

There were murmurs of assent.

"For today, we're all going to take part in set design," she said.

"My dad's going to do that," Landon said.

"He's going to supervise," Emily corrected, "but you boys are going to do all the work."

The question was, where was Dev?

She would never have chosen to get him involved, given how awkward things were between them. But due to Landon's innocent plea for his involvement, there was no choice and no way to graciously refuse his help. The other teachers had been thrilled to know the new janitor was willing to take on this sort of work, and Emily had the feeling that Dev was going to be a set designer for many productions to come.

Which was great, but she had to figure out

how to get through the first play while working closely with him.

Without thinking continually about how wonderful it had been to kiss him.

She'd beaten herself up about that since practically the moment after it had happened. She should have known better. What had she been thinking, snuggling up so close with him? What had she expected to take place when she let things get physical?

A part of her was even glad. She'd had that one kiss with a man she admired and cared for, those few minutes of dreaming about being a couple with Dev. That wonderful sense of protection and caring.

She'd have it to cling to, to keep forever.

That was why she had done it, she supposed. After the day of grief about her lost child, and struggling with her mother, she simply hadn't had the willpower left to resist his magnetic pull. She hadn't wanted to. She'd wanted the closeness, the warmth, the caring.

A stronger, better woman would have kept that invisible barrier between them, the barrier of "we're just friends." Dev wouldn't have broken through it without encouragement from her. He was a man of honor; she knew that about him just from their short acquaintance.

But no, she'd cuddled right up against him in

that beautiful place, surrounded by God's majestic creation. She'd craved the comfort of his nearness, his strength.

And because she'd given in to that craving, she now had to keep total distance from him. She'd had to be rude and push him away, hurtfully.

It was more kind in the end, she reminded herself.

Dev strode into the multipurpose hall then, tall and muscular, his sleeves rolled up. He looked harassed as he came over to the table of squabbling, chattering boys. "Sorry I'm late," he said to Emily, keeping his voice low. "Vandalism incident in the upstairs restroom."

"Oh, no, is everything okay?"

He flashed a smile. "Caught the perps in time. They're up there scrubbing, supervised by Stan."

"Oh, good." She started to smile at him and then remembered that she had to keep her distance. She cleared her throat. "Are you ready to get the boys started on sets, or do you need a minute?"

He forked a hand through his hair and looked away from her, as if he'd also only just remembered that their friendship held a big dose of awkwardness now. "I, uh, I'm ready. Tell me what you want."

She pulled out her laptop and found photos

from other productions. He leaned over her, looking at them. "Yeah. We can do that." He pointed. "But you want to keep it simple, right? So maybe that would work better." He pointed at another example.

"Perfect." She could smell his cologne, something woodsy. She remembered that from when they'd kissed, and it swept her back to that moment. Her skin heated. "Let's go up to the stage."

And she'd better bring the boys along to keep things from getting personal between them.

It worked. Dev scouted the area, thought for a minute and then turned and knelt to talk to the boys, describing what they'd do. "We're going to need older boys to do some sawing and hammering. Younger boys to paint," he finished.

The boys paid attention to what he said. They liked him already, she could tell. The school was small enough that everyone knew everyone, and even though Dev had only been on the job a little over a month, he seemed to have met every kid in the school. She was impressed that he knew all the names already and had even noticed that Camden was good at art and that Chip spent extra time in shop class.

He took three of the strongest boys with him to gather supplies, and Emily worked with the others, showing them clips from a video of another performance of the play. Dev and his crew returned with carts loaded with plywood and paint and tools. More quickly than Emily would have expected, he had all of them occupied with age-appropriate tasks. He was gruff with them, businesslike, but they didn't seem to mind; they rose to the occasion and worked hard to earn his occasional flash of a smile.

Emily was surprised and impressed to see this side of him. He was really good with the kids. Was there anything this man couldn't do?

Since he had them well under control, she was able to pull out one boy at a time. She had the stronger students read for the lead roles and showed those who didn't read well a video sequence to act out. Chip showed a real propensity for slapstick, just as she'd suspected from his clowning around in reading class, so she assigned him a major comic role.

In between kids, she watched Dev work. That was okay, wasn't it? He didn't know. And she liked seeing him kneel beside the younger boys, teaching them to paint properly or hammer a nail. She was impressed at the way he stopped an argument from escalating with a few quiet words.

They listened to him, and part of it was the fact that they needed and benefited from male role models, and that Dev was still new to them. But another man could have easily blown that advantage and chaos would have ensued, because these boys could be difficult.

Dev held their attention without any trouble. Impressive.

When it was almost time to go, she suggested that they clean up and then stood near Dev as the boys worked. Honesty compelled her to compliment him. "You're really good working with these boys. Are you sure you weren't a teacher in another life?"

He snorted. "No way. Not the academic type."

"You work with them well."

He shrugged. "I was like them, growing up. One of the so-called troublemakers, so I don't judge them the way some of the teachers do."

Interested despite her better judgment, she studied him. "Why were you a troublemaker?"

He shrugged. "Moved around a lot, in the system. Didn't do too well in school. The usual reasons." He glanced at her quickly and then away.

"That must have been hard." She wanted to know more. Wanted to hear about what it had been like to move from home to home, school to school.

Her phone buzzed, and she pulled it out and looked at it. When she saw the number, her heart sank. "I have to take this," she said, "but it'll be quick. Sorry. Can you…" She gestured at the boys.

"I've got them. Go ahead."

She walked away and gathered her patience to speak with her late husband's mother. "Hi, Suzanne."

The woman was already crying. "Did you forget that it's time to start working on the race?"

Emily sat down at a table, her mood plummeting. "We said last year was going to be the final one."

"We talked about that. But I can't stand it." Suzanne was sobbing heavily now. "I can't… I just can't…forget him. I know it's easier for you…"

Don't react. Emily reminded herself to take deep breaths. Lady came and leaned against her. For several minutes, she listened to Suzanne cry and gasp.

When her mother-in-law finally sputtered to near silence, Emily spoke. "Is John there?"

"No," Suzanne said. Audible breaths. "No, he's golfing. Golfing, and me in this state!"

Emily mentally congratulated her former father-in-law for taking care of himself. She put a hand on Lady's curly head and rubbed and scratched the dog behind her ears. Lady slowly sank to the floor, leaning against Emily's hand.

"I w-w-want to do it again, one more time," Suzanne quivered. "Can't we do it one more time?"

One more memorial race for her late husband. Could she manage it?

Of course she could. But last year, the race had only raised $200 for the charity designated, and the number of participants had been embarrassingly small. John, her father-in-law, had barely found time to announce the race to his work colleagues. It wasn't that he didn't care, or miss his son, but he'd resumed the rest of his life.

Suzanne, although she had always expressed enthusiasm for the race, had done less and less of the actual work each year. Last year it had fallen entirely on Emily to organize, fundraise and execute an event for the husband she'd struggled to stay with.

Naturally, she'd felt horrible about his death, especially when the cause of the fire had been determined to be her mother's leaving food cooking on the stove. The fact that Mitch had fallen asleep drunk, that he'd told her he'd changed the smoke alarm batteries when he'd really just pulled the old ones out—none of that carelessness meant that he deserved to have his life cut short.

She'd missed him, too. Maybe more, because their relationship had been troubled and there hadn't been time to work anything out. No time to talk through her own anger that he hadn't been alert enough to save their child. No time for him to explain. No time to laugh together, to make up.

In the end—and this was what Suzanne and John had jumped on—it was Emily who'd chosen to go out with friends, leaving their grandson and Mitch and Emily's mother alone.

The guilt of it swirled up in her. "I'll think about it, Suzanne, but please don't get your hopes up. Let's also consider just making a donation to the fire department instead."

"But that wouldn't have the same meaning..." Suzanne talked on, and Emily looked at the stage. Dev was still working with the boys, but he kept glancing her way. Probably wondering why she was talking on the phone rather than fulfilling her responsibilities.

"Look, I have to go," she said, cutting off the stream of words. "I'll be in touch within the next few days about the race, but please think about alternatives."

"I guess I'll have to contact some of Mitch's friends," she said, her voice rising toward anger. "I'm sure *they'd* be glad to help."

Not really, Emily wanted to say. Mitch's friends weren't exactly volunteer-of-the-year types, or at least, they hadn't been. Emily had never gotten along with them.

"I'm at work, and I really do have to go,"

Emily said, and when Suzanne kept talking, she ended the call.

Which would infuriate the woman, and understandably so, but there wasn't much to be done about it. Suzanne didn't understand things like jobs, because she'd never had one. She'd had everything go her way in life—until she'd lost her son and grandson, of course—but those early advantages hadn't made her happy. She'd provided the same environment for her son, and it hadn't served him well, either, though he'd certainly been handsome and charming enough to sweep Emily off her feet.

She shoved her phone in her pocket, gave Lady a final head rub and went up the stairs to the stage. "Thanks for taking over," she said to Dev. "I think we can start them cleaning up."

Dev put two fingers to his mouth and whistled. "Okay, everyone. Lids on paint cans, tools back in their containers. Everything can be stacked against the far wall. Landon and Chip, you're on sweeping duty. Brooms on the cart."

Emily was stunned at his efficiency. "You're good at that!"

He laughed. "Years of experience telling people what to do. I've headed up teams at a couple of jobs I had. Are you okay?" he added, his face sobering. "Seemed like you had a rough phone call."

"I did," she said. But she didn't want to talk about Mitch to Dev, didn't want to speak ill of him or his parents. "Just a flash from the past. It'll all work out fine."

At least, she hoped so. As soon as she'd ended the call, she'd regretted not just saying a firm no right away. Doing the race again would be a mistake. She made a vow to herself that she'd contribute $200 to the fire department as soon as she'd gotten her car fixed.

It was a way to ease her conscience, and so maybe a little selfish, but it would do some good.

The trouble was, Suzanne had a vindictive side. If Emily didn't fall into line with what she wanted, Suzanne would undoubtedly attempt to make her pay.

But Emily was finally getting stronger. She wasn't going to let a troubled woman guide her life.

She just hoped the retaliation wouldn't be too swift and severe.

When they'd gotten the boys off to their house parents—Landon going along, so he could share dinner with some of his new friends—Dev looked around for Emily, only to see her walking rapidly away, toward their cabins.

She didn't want to spend time with him. That was obvious.

Also obvious was that the phone call she'd received had been upsetting. Was still upsetting, if the slump of her shoulders was any indication.

He thought about following her, pushing her to tell him what was wrong. They were supposed to be friends.

Only the friendship had gotten overcomplicated by the fact that they'd shared that kiss. That they'd pushed it over the line from friendship into something more.

Dev wished it hadn't happened, because it meant that he couldn't be a true friend to Emily now without having it colored with a desire for romance.

He also felt motivated to try and make something work between them.

They'd been good together this afternoon, working with the boys. He'd enjoyed it, had been impressed with the efficient way she'd kept the project moving ahead and sympathetically matched up some of the boys with roles that fit their skills. Never once making anyone feel lacking or bad about it.

And she'd seemed sincere in admiring the work he was doing with the boys, too.

Landon was ecstatic. He loved the idea of being in a play, loved working on the set and, most of all, loved the new friends he was making. Unlike at his old school, here he wasn't ostracized for having trouble with reading. Everyone here had problems of one kind or another, which meant they didn't judge quite so harshly as mainstream kids.

Landon also really, really liked Emily. For the first time, Dev wondered whether Landon's effort to get Dev to work on the show had included an element of junior matchmaking.

If so, maybe the kid had a point. Maybe Dev and Emily would make a good couple.

But Dev had something to overcome first.

He looked back at the school and noticed that Ashley Green's office light was on. Before he could second-guess the idea, he went back inside and tapped on the half-closed door of the principal's office. "Hey, Ashley?"

"Dev." She looked up, smiled and beckoned him in. "How'd the rehearsal go?"

He admired the woman for how she seemed genuinely welcoming to everyone who came into her office, even if they were interrupting her work, and also for how she seemed to know everything that went on in the school. "It went well," he said. "Kids had a good time."

"Good." She studied him. "Sit down and tell me what's up. You're not one to drop in for no reason."

He nodded. "I... I wanted to talk to you about something."

"Landon?" she asked. "I hear he's improving, although we're still keeping it open whether he repeats the year or not. He was pretty far behind."

"I know, and we're working on that." He skimmed his damp hands down the sides of his jeans. "It's not Landon, it's...it's me."

She nodded and waited.

"I, well, I have a problem, and I need your help with it." He sucked in a deep breath, trying without success to calm his racing heart. "I need... I need help with my own reading—" He rushed over the words, not wanting to give her time to react. "And I don't want to distract Emily from Landon. Is there another teacher I could pay to tutor me?"

Underneath the fear and the shame, he felt the slightest flicker of hope.

He shouldn't feel hopeful, because he was telling his boss something that could probably get him fired. A smarter man would've called some anonymous literacy hotline.

But there was something about the Bright Tomorrows school that encouraged optimism. Maybe it was the photos of former students that lined the school office, some wearing suits, some in humbler work clothes, but all of them smiling, looking proud.

It gave you the feeling that maybe you could succeed, make yourself and others proud, too.

She studied him. "I suspected you struggled with reading," she said.

Dev stared at her. "You *did*?"

"I did." She twirled a pencil in her hands. "I'm a reading teacher by background, too, and I noticed the signs. You always forget your glasses, so someone else has to read to you. You talk things through rather than writing them down. And you have a very sharp memory. You've had to, I'm sure, to achieve this level of professional success with weak reading skills."

He blew out a breath and leaned back in his chair. He was embarrassed, but he also felt strangely relieved. There was something tiring about having to hide his situation from everyone. It was good to have a person who knew.

"I think you're right that Emily doesn't have time," she said. "And…my guess is that there are other reasons her tutoring you wouldn't be a good idea."

Dev met her eyes steadily. "If you're worried about us getting to be too close of friends—"

"No," she interrupted, raising a hand like a stop sign. "If I were worried, I'd say so. I have confidence that the two of you are goodhearted, discreet individuals."

He opened his mouth to tell her there was nothing between them and then shut it again. There *was* something between them. Something strange, and probably doomed, but something.

"If I could make a suggestion," she said. "I'd like to work with you on a few tests to find out what you're dealing with. Have you ever been diagnosed with dyslexia?"

"No. No way."

She lifted an eyebrow. "It's not a disgrace, it's a disability. And there's a chance your son may have it. That came up in our meeting about Landon this week."

"It *did*?" Why hadn't Emily told him?

Then again, things hadn't been exactly friendly between them.

"It was in the letter Emily sent home… Oh." She gave a rueful half smile, and he saw the realization hit her: Dev couldn't read the school papers Landon brought home. Of course, he did his best to puzzle out the meaning of the ones that looked important, but inevitably, he missed things. Like that Landon should be tested for dyslexia.

"It tends to run in families," Ashley went on. "If you were never tested yourself—"

"I don't have dyslexia. I'm just…slow. With

reading, writing, things like that." As he uttered the words, he flashed back to the boy he'd been. *Slow.* He'd heard the word jostled around as he'd been transferred from school to school, foster home to foster home.

He was just slow.

"I don't think you're *just slow*, Dev," she said. "I've seen you fix a boiler without directions, mix up cement without measuring, just by feel. You know the name of every kid in the school. You've developed superior coping skills, some of the best I've seen."

He waved off her words and the small surge of pride they engendered in him. "I think, after seeing the way Landon's working, that I could improve. I can read," he emphasized quickly, his face reddening. "Just not well."

"I agree that you can improve," she said. "And if you'll give me, say, three one-hour sessions, I can help you figure out next steps."

"Wow." Could it really be that simple? "Are you sure you have time to work with me?"

She leaned forward. "I do, because I care about my employees. You have a lot of potential, Dev. It would be to the school's benefit for you to reach it."

Dev's face heated.

She waved a hand. "I'm sorry if I sound like I'm speaking to a kid. Career educator. And obviously, I can't continue working with you beyond some initial tests. For one thing, my reading certification is expired. And there's the time factor. But there are some terrific online teachers who could work with you on a regular basis. You're motivated. You'll make fast progress."

Dev blew out a breath and leaned back. "I... Wow. I never really came clean with anyone before, at least not for a while." He'd admitted the truth to Roxy, and it hadn't turned out well. "I don't want to miss work hours, but I notice you're usually here early. Could I come in before the school day starts? Maybe while Landon is getting tutored?"

She pulled out a calendar and they set it up. "I'm glad you came to me, Dev," she said. "This is going to be a big, positive change in your life, and I'm impressed you're ready and willing to make it."

"Thanks." Dev left with a bounce in his step. He hoped Ashley was right. If she was, coming to Bright Tomorrows might turn out to be the best thing for him as well as for Landon.

And if he could get up to par with reading... He looked toward Emily's cottage. Maybe, just maybe, he'd get up the confidence to try to convince Emily to explore a relationship, too.

Chapter Thirteen

❧

"You did great today!" Emily hugged Landon on Friday morning after their tutoring session. "Now, pack up your stuff while I make you one of my speedy egg sandwiches." He'd seen her eating one when he'd arrived, doughnut in hand, and had said it looked good. She'd offered to make him one as long as he worked hard in tutoring, and he had.

It was just a simple English muffin topped with an egg and cheese, but she found herself humming as she sizzled butter in a small pan and then cracked an egg into it. Landon, having quickly stuffed his books into his backpack, was on the floor with Lady.

Could she be blamed if she pretended, just for a few minutes, that she was Landon's mom?

Outside was cold enough that her breath had

made clouds when she'd gone out on her porch to welcome Landon.

Dev had stood on his porch, too, and had given her a wave, but he hadn't come over. Which was totally fine. Good, even. They'd be spending so much time together between random school day encounters and working on the play. There was no reason they needed to have a conversation first thing in the morning.

The muffin popped up in the toaster. She poured Landon a glass of orange juice and then built the muffin sandwich. "Here you go," she said. "Eat fast. We need to get going."

"I'm gonna get an A on my word problem homework," Landon bragged as they walked to school. He briefly got distracted by a magpie that landed on a fencepost beside them, chattering and scolding. He jumped and yelled until the big bird flew up to land on a bare aspen branch. "Then I'm gonna get an A on the test!" He frowned. "Or a B. Bs are okay."

"They sure are," Emily said, amused by him. They walked into the school lobby, where a few day students waited for the first bell.

"Let's see which signs you can read," Emily suggested. "I'm guessing you can read this one."

Landon looked up and frowned. "That's too long."

"You can sound it out," she encouraged. She covered all but the first two letters. "*R* and long *e*."

"Ree?" he said.

"Yes! Now here's the hard part." She covered both ends of the word. "Remember we talked about blending sounds? There's an *SP* here, like in…"

"Sports!" He'd struggled with that word this morning and figured it out.

"Good. But this has an *e*…" They went on, working through the long word, and she was proud of how Landon stuck with it. He would have kicked the wall or run away just three weeks ago.

Groups of kids were arriving from the residence houses. As the lobby got more crowded, the office door opened, and Ashley emerged to give her daily greeting to the students.

Dev was with her.

They were both laughing. They'd been in her office together.

Ashley was beautiful, tall and blonde and slim, her skin perfect. She had a ready smile and was already well-liked by the teachers.

Apparently, she was well-liked by Dev, too.

A primal *nooooo* formed instantly in her mind, and she actually took a step toward the pair.

And then she stopped herself. What was she

thinking? She couldn't have Dev. She couldn't have any relationship; she'd made that decision on a cold night six years ago, so choked with tears and smoke and guilt that she could barely breathe.

"Dad! Look what I can read!" Landon rushed to Dev and tugged him over by the hand. "Look at this long word. It says, 'Ree-spect-ful.' Respectful."

"Wow, that's great," Dev said.

Ashley had followed them. "Good job," she said warmly.

Landon saw Chip and rushed over to him, leaving Dev, Emily and Ashley standing together.

"Early-morning meeting, huh?" Emily could have kicked herself as soon as she blurted it out, but she wanted to know.

Dev chuckled awkwardly. "Something like that."

"Well, I have a school to run," Ashley said. "See you soon."

Did she look at Dev in a special way? Did she mean something specific by *see you soon*? Did the two of them have plans?

She felt like putting an arm around Dev, claiming him in front of everyone, shouting out that he'd kissed *her*, not Ashley.

Although maybe he'd kissed Ashley, too,

during their "something like" an early-morning meeting.

"When you get the chance, I'd like to get an update on Landon's progress," Dev said.

"Sure. Of course. He's doing well, but I can give you the details. In fact," she blurted out, "we could go to dinner after tonight's rehearsal."

He studied her for a moment while her face heated.

"Okay," he said slowly, "we can do that. Pretty sure Landon has a movie night at the residence houses tonight."

"Great! Got to go, get set up for the day!" She escaped to the library, her heart pounding.

Why on earth had she just asked Dev out on what amounted to a date?

Why had Emily asked Dev to go to dinner?

Okay, granted, he'd asked her to update him on Landon's progress. And granted, he was more than happy to see her outside work, and that probably showed.

But she'd made it clear she didn't want *that* kind of relationship. Had she changed her mind?

As he held the door for her at Café Aztec in Little Mesa, he couldn't help noticing her pretty dress, different than the practical clothes she usually wore to school. The rose color of it brought out the pink in her cheeks, which looked pinker than usual. Was she wearing makeup or was she blushing?

Once they were seated, she gave him a shy smile. "I didn't realize it would be this formal," she said. "I've never been here before. It was out of my..." She trailed off, her cheeks getting pinker. "Anyway, I wanted to try it, and I'm glad you were game."

"It's not very often that I have an evening without Landon," he said, "or that a pretty lady asks me to dinner." When she blushed harder and looked away, he could have kicked himself.

She didn't mean it like a date. She meant it like a meeting. Maybe. Probably.

"Emily Carver, is that you?" An older lady stopped by their table. She wore some kind of big, long cape, purple and blue, and a lot of jewelry.

"Hi, Mrs. Armstrong." Emily's voice sounded strained, and her smile looked forced. "How are you?"

"I'm well, dear." She looked at Dev appraisingly.

"Mrs. Armstrong, this is Dev McCarthy."

"Nice to meet you." Dev started to stand.

"Likewise, and don't stand up, I'm just saying hello," she said. "Emily, I'm glad to see that you're recovering so well." She gave Dev another glance, then swept off, her jewelry clanking.

Emily watched her go, frowning.

"Not a friend?" he asked.

"No. She's a friend of…my former mother-in-law. And I'm sure she's already on the phone with Suzanne, letting her know I'm out with a man."

He narrowed his eyes. "Your husband's been gone for a while, right?"

She nodded. "Six years. But for Suzanne, it's like yesterday. She'll be furious." She bit her lip. "This isn't good."

Dev studied her. She looked so worried, maybe almost ready to cry, and he didn't get it. "She doesn't have a say in your life, does she? After all this time?"

"She shouldn't, but…it's complicated."

The waiter came over and asked about drinks, and they both ordered iced tea. "We haven't even looked at the menu yet," Emily apologized in Spanish.

"*No hay problema.* Take your time."

And here they were at the most difficult part of any restaurant outing. Some places had pictures on the menu, which helped, but not this one. The words on it seemed to blur together. "What are you having?" he asked.

"I'm not sure. So many choices. What are you thinking about?"

Sweat dripped down his back. "No clue. I'll ask about specials when the waiter comes back."

He hated being this way, having to pretend all the time. And in fact, he and Ashley had spent a little time talking about that today: how he shouldn't be ashamed; how there was a good possibility he had dyslexia, which was a disability; how it was like a person who used a wheelchair or couldn't hear well—you wouldn't blame them for it.

"Yeah," he'd said, "but most adults can read better than I can, right? Even if they're dyslexic?"

After he'd told her about his background, she hadn't sugarcoated it. "Your social workers and teachers and foster parents did you a disservice, not helping you figure out why school was a struggle. Most people have more advantages, frankly."

"But can I learn?" It was a pathetic question, but he had to know.

"Of course!" She'd seemed shocked that he would doubt it. "You'll learn, and quickly, once we're certain of a diagnosis and get you into a program."

"How quickly?" he'd asked.

She'd lifted her hands, palms up. "Everyone's different, but I would think you'd be reading well in a couple of years, maximum."

He'd covered his reaction, but inside, he'd groaned. In a couple of years, he'd be forty-two years old. Landon would be finishing elementary school, maybe here, maybe somewhere else.

In a couple of years, Emily would probably be married to some guy of equal intelligence and education.

"Have you decided?" the waiter asked, breaking into Dev's thoughts.

"What are your specials?" he asked after Emily had ordered, and the waiter recited them. He heard one that sounded good, and told the man he'd take that, and the difficult moment was over.

But he was thinking. Maybe he didn't have to wait a couple of years. Maybe he could tell Emily the truth, and soon.

"You wanted to talk about Landon," she said now. "He does seem to have a reading disability, probably dyslexia. I think I mentioned that in my note. Does that run in the family?"

And he was sweating again. "Um… I… I don't know. No one ever talked about it."

"It can sometimes go undiagnosed," she said. "Can he get past it?"

"Of course!" She displayed the same confidence about Landon that Ashley had displayed about him. "It's a matter of showing him strategies to recognize words and sounds. Partly, it's getting him to slow down enough to try to decode words. He's smart, and he's gotten away with guessing so far, I imagine."

Dev liked hearing that Landon was smart. He'd always thought so. "He has a wicked good memory. He can recite the dialogue from any movie he watches. I'll get an earful of *Monster-Man* tomorrow, I'm sure."

She smiled. "That's a strength we can use. I've already ordered him audio versions of his textbooks. Once he hears them, I'm sure his test grades will shoot up."

"Are there audio versions available?"

She nodded. "Yes, and the school has to provide them once his disability is identified."

"Great." He was thrilled to already see a path forward for Landon. "So you think he can pass third grade?"

"I do. He knows a lot of the material just from listening in class. It's a matter of helping him learn to write out answers. And meanwhile, as soon as he has a diagnosis, he can take some tests orally."

"Wow." He wondered what school would have been like for him if he'd had those kind of supports in place.

Their food came then, and they dug in. Dev enjoyed his meal—delicious, authentic Mexican food—but even more, he enjoyed watching Emily enjoy it.

They chatted about the school, and about local hikes they'd both like to do in the summer, and about the Denver Broncos' chances for another good year. She offered him a taste of her *chile rellenos*, and he shared his *posole*, and it all felt natural. Fun. Nice.

He'd half worried that, on a social occasion, he and Emily wouldn't have anything to talk about, or that dinner out would be awkward. But just like at work, or on their car rides to visit her mom, they got along as if they were old friends.

He felt like a kid who was unwrapping a present he hadn't expected to receive. He'd known he was attracted to Emily, but that wasn't enough for a relationship. He'd figured she was out of his league, intellectually, but they actually got pretty deep talking about the pastor's sermon last week, and he held his own.

Plus, according to both Ashley and Emily, reading problems didn't necessarily mean you weren't smart. They could just mean your brain worked differently.

Still, the thought of how Roxy had mocked him about his inability to read well made him shrink from telling Emily the truth. And if he couldn't tell the truth, then they couldn't have a relationship; it was that simple.

So he shouldn't be feeling excited. A better man would put his feelings on hold, keep it friendly and no-touch.

The problem was that Emily looked so sweet and pretty, sweeter and prettier than any woman Dev had ever known. And as pretty as she was, that wasn't the main thing about her; she was a good person inside, too. No wonder he felt that push to get closer.

When the check arrived, he reached for it at the same time she did. "I'll get this," he said.

"No, it's okay, I'll pay my share."

"Your money's no good here." He tried to make a joke of it, but the truth was, he wanted to pay. Treating her would make him happy, and besides, he knew money was short for her.

Paying also made it feel more like a date, for him, at least.

After a little more protesting, she let him pay, and when they walked out together, he touched the small of her back, then took her hand.

The whole time he was yelling at himself. *Don't do it. Don't hold her hand. Don't raise expectations.*

He didn't listen. Not as he held her hand on the way out, and not as he opened the door for her, and not as he drove them home.

When they got there, the air felt pregnant with promise. He wasn't sure she felt the same way, but for him, he could hardly breathe for wanting to pull her into his arms.

She looked at him, her gaze direct. "Thank you for dinner, Dev," she said. "I appreciate it, but I won't ask again."

"Why's that?" He turned off the truck and climbed out, then came around to get her door, giving both of them a chance to think.

He helped her down but dropped her hand immediately. He wasn't going to push himself on her. It was wiser to keep a distance if this wasn't going anywhere.

And until he shared the truth about himself, it *couldn't* go anywhere. His head knew that, but it was having a hard time convincing his heart.

She put her hands on her hips and faced him. "There's something between us. We're both adults, and we know what we're feeling isn't the same as just friends." She blushed, laughed a little. "Well, me, anyway. But I have too many issues to pursue it."

"It's not you, it's me? Is that what you're saying?" He tried to keep it light, but the words came out sounding hurt.

She sighed, and then she did reach for his hand, held it in both of hers. "Oh, Dev, you're such a great guy, and any woman would be blessed to have you as a boyfriend. It's just... I'm not who you think I am." She squeezed his hand and then dropped it, turned, squared her shoulders and walked to the house.

I'm not who you think I am, either, he wanted to say.

He didn't say it. But he did think that maybe, maybe they could wait for each other. Maybe be friends until they were ready to be more.

A little spark of hope lit in him, a kind of pilot light. He'd keep it burning and see what happened.

He went to pick up Landon with a light heart.

Chapter Fourteen

Saturday morning, Emily gathered her gardening things and went outside. At this high elevation, it was a little early to plant spring flowers, but she wanted to prepare the ground. Soon enough, the risk of frost would pass, true spring would come and she could plant all the colorful flowers she loved.

She wet the ground with the garden hose and pulled up a few weeds. Though the air was cool, the sun warmed her shoulders. Lady chased squirrels and leaped at butterflies, looking as happy as Emily felt inside.

The date with Dev last night had been wonderful. Of course, it hadn't really been a date, but it had felt like one. He'd insisted on paying for the meal. He'd held her hand and opened doors for her. He'd acted like he cared, and by now, she knew him well enough to know he wouldn't fake that.

He cared for her!

She wrapped her arms around herself, smiling at nobody, feeling breathless. He cared. Dev McCarthy cared for *her*.

And despite the past six years she'd spent saying she was fine, just fine focusing on work and dodging a social life, she could admit now that she wanted that for herself. She wanted to care and be cared for again.

Like the newly fertile ground she was digging and tilling, springtime was coming inside her, too. She wasn't quite ready yet, but the possibility of new life, new love, was in reach.

Maybe she and Dev could give a relationship a try.

The sound of a car coming up the road this early surprised her. "Lady," she called, and the poodle ran to her side.

She expected the big, dark luxury sedan to drive on past, but it stopped in front of her cottage. She stood and squinted, and her heart sank.

Her former in-laws were inside.

As they climbed out, her good feelings seeped away like air from a slow-leaking tire. Guilt and hurt and anger churned inside her.

She stood as John opened the passenger door for Suzanne.

And then they marched toward her, side by side, not smiling.

"Is it true what I heard," Suzanne asked, "that you were out on a date with some man, practically on the anniversary of Mitchell's death?"

Emily blew out a breath and stripped off her gardening gloves. Lady leaned against her, and she put down a hand to touch the dog's curly head. "Hi, Suzanne. John. I wasn't expecting you this morning."

"Well?" Suzanne's voice rose to a higher pitch. "Is it true?"

Involuntarily, Emily glanced over at Dev's place, then wished she hadn't. She looked back at her in-laws. "Would you like to come in?"

Suzanne planted her hands on her hips. "I was *going* to talk to you about the memorial 5-K, but now I see why you're not interested. Why you don't care anymore!" Her voice got louder, punching out each word.

Next door, Dev walked out onto his porch, Landon beside him. He didn't even pretend he wasn't paying attention; he actually came to the side of the porch and looked over, arms crossed.

He was so handsome. So thoughtful and kind.

So out of her league...but, she reminded herself, he seemed to care about her anyway.

Landon came partway down the porch steps, stopping at a quiet word from his father. "Hi, Lady," he called.

Lady's tail thumped, but she stayed by Emily's side.

John turned to look at Dev and Landon. "What did your friend say he looked like?" he asked Suzanne. Before she could answer, he glared at Emily. "Is this the man?"

The questions and emotions swirled around her, and she bit her lip and kept a hand on Lady.

"You okay, Emily?" Dev called across the lawns.

"I'm fine," she said, nodding at him. "Everything's okay." Obviously untrue statements, but what she meant was, *don't come over, I'll handle it.*

He seemed to get the message, because he nodded once and went inside.

Which was what she needed to get John and Suzanne to do, if they insisted on staying. She didn't need an audience for their scolding. "Why don't you both come inside? I'll make coffee."

Suzanne ignored the suggestion. "After you caused our son's death, you dare to go on with your life? I'll never go on with my life!" She wiped tears from under her eyes and held out a hand, and John gave her a clean white handkerchief. He'd always carried one, even before

Mitch's death, because Suzanne's meltdowns were frequent and teary.

"We didn't just lose our son," he added, putting an arm around Suzanne. "Our grandson, as well. Our only grandson."

Emily squeezed her eyes shut as waves of guilt crashed over her. They were articulating the worst things she told herself, on her worst days, and it was hard to hear them said aloud. And a shallow part of her worried that Dev would hear them blaming her. Both Suzanne and John had voices that carried.

And she felt deep, deep sympathy for them, she really did. She of all people knew how devastating it was to lose a child.

"We've been talking to some of Mitch's friends, your mutual friends," John said. "They had an interesting perspective."

"We hadn't been in touch with them since the tragedy, but because you didn't seem like you wanted to work on the race, I reached out to them." Suzanne's voice quavered.

Emily felt her shoulders tightening more, which hadn't even seemed possible.

"They think you knew he'd had too much to drink," John said, "and yet you went out anyway."

"I got my mom to come over and help, in case…" Emily trailed off, knowing that to defend herself was fruitless. But it was the truth. She hadn't known Mitch was already drinking that night, didn't think he had been, but she knew his habits. That was why she'd asked her mom to come as backup.

"Your mom has Alzheimer's! She caused the fire!" Suzanne's voice rose at the end, her face a dangerous shade of pink.

John tightened his arm around Suzanne's shoulder. "Criminal negligence, even if the police wouldn't call it that."

Emily sank down onto the steps. Their words felt like physical blows, pounding her head and shoulders, crushing her.

Lady trotted up the steps and sat beside her at the top, leaning hard against her.

Alongside the pain John and Suzanne were causing, a little anger flickered. It had been six years, six painful years, since the horrible incident had occurred, since her own life had been ruined. John and Suzanne had always hinted at these blameful attitudes, but they'd never been this explicit before. Probably because she'd always meekly done everything they'd asked of her. She'd never stepped out of line.

"I don't know how you dare show your face in public, laughing and enjoying yourself with another man." Suzanne looked daggers at her.

"Does *he* know what you did?" John asked, pointing at Dev's house.

She couldn't help looking over there. Dev was nowhere in sight, but Landon knelt on the porch, a couple of forgotten action figures at his side, his expression distressed.

She'd caused that. Here she'd pretended Landon was her son, let herself imagine Dev as her boyfriend. She didn't deserve either.

"You should be ashamed of yourself," Suzanne shouted and then broke down sobbing again.

"Disgusting." John put an arm around Suzanne and guided her back to the car.

As they drove away in a spray of gravel and dust, Emily sat still, arms wrapped around her knees. If she moved, she might shatter like fragile glass.

Lady nudged at her, but even the dog's gentle touch didn't lessen the pain she felt.

It was true, what they'd said. The disaster she'd experienced was her own fault. She needed to go back to focusing solely on her work. Stop trying to have fun like a normal person who hadn't done anything wrong.

The penance for her sin would last a lifetime, and even that wouldn't be enough to make up for it.

There was a sound from next door, and concern for Landon made her look over that way. But it wasn't Landon; it was Dev.

Relief loosened the tension in her body and she turned a little toward him, putting an arm around Lady for strength.

Dev wasn't smiling as he walked toward her. "Is all that true?" he asked, his voice abrupt. "What they said. Is that how it happened?"

"I..." She swallowed, nodded. "Basically, yes."

"You were at fault?"

Shame churned inside her. "I... I don't like to admit it. But yes."

He studied her for a long moment. His face was stiff and still, but his eyes seemed to burn through her. And then he spoke. "Landon doesn't need that kind of influence."

"What?" That was the last thing she'd expected him to say.

"I'm taking Landon out of tutoring."

She stood, distressed. "But he needs consistency to pass his final tests."

"There are other teachers, online teachers," he said. "Maybe even Ashley."

Ashley. Perfect, innocent Ashley.

There was a noise from the bushes surrounding Dev's porch, and then Landon burst out. He'd obviously been eavesdropping. "Dad! I don't want another tutor, I want Ms. Carver!"

"We need to make a change," Dev said, his voice gentling a little as he looked down at his son.

"I don't want a change!" Landon started to cry.

Emily's heart felt like it was reaching out of her chest toward the little boy. She took a step toward him, but Dev held out a quelling hand.

"I want Ms. Carver to teach me." Landon's voice shook with tears.

Lady whined.

"Go," she ordered quietly, gesturing toward Landon. The dog didn't need a second command. She ran to Landon and nudged him, and he knelt down and hugged the dog, still crying.

"Come on, Landon. Let go of the dog." Dev's voice was flat and gruff.

"I don't—"

"Call her off," Dev said to Emily.

"No," Landon sobbed.

"Now," Dev said.

Her throat felt impossibly tight, but she pushed out the words. "Lady. Come."

The dog hesitated a moment, then wiggled out of Landon's grip and trotted back to Emily.

"Come on," Dev said. He put an arm around Landon's shoulders and ushered him inside.

As she listened to Landon's sobs, Emily's own heart seemed to turn to sand.

* * *

Dev spent the rest of the weekend trying to manage Landon's emotions and to stifle his own.

He'd built Emily up into something she wasn't, and now both he and Landon were paying the price. Dev was kicking himself for not realizing what was happening: Landon had gotten way too attached to Emily and to Lady. Losing one meant losing both.

But if he let Landon continue to work with Emily—which meant not only getting tutored, but getting hugs and hot breakfasts and a dog to play with—Landon would learn the lesson that it was okay to cover things up, avoid responsibility, lie about what you'd done. That was what had started him down the wrong road before.

Why hadn't he done his due diligence before agreeing to have Emily tutor his son? After his experience with his wife, he should have known better.

Landon fussed and whined and threw things, reverting to the unhappy kid he'd been under his mother's care. Which served Dev right, and he tried to make things better by skipping church and taking Landon fishing, but Landon was too easily frustrated and neither of them caught anything. Dev was almost relieved when an afternoon storm blew in so he could have an excuse to take Landon home early.

Flashes of Emily's devastated face kept intruding into his anger. Of course, she must feel terrible about what she'd done. She wasn't a monster, and what mother wouldn't grieve hard at the fact that she'd caused her child's death?

He felt sorry for her; he did. He just didn't want to be involved with that kind of person. Couldn't risk Landon's safety getting close to someone that careless and thoughtless, that self-absorbed. She'd known her husband had been drinking, and she'd gone out anyway. She'd left her son in the care of someone who couldn't handle the responsibility because she had Alzheimer's.

Criminal negligence. He'd gotten involved with someone who had been criminally negligent toward her own child.

And there was the crux of it: Dev had gotten involved. He'd started to hope that, once he managed some of his own deficits, he'd be able to build something with Emily, or with the woman he'd thought she was.

He'd been stupid, which was his trademark. He'd made another idiotic mistake, and now Landon was miserable because of it.

When Monday morning came, he was relieved, until he realized that Landon was going to miss tutoring, which meant that Dev would miss his session with Ashley. Not only that, but there was a rehearsal tonight, and he was supposed to work with Emily on the play. He committed himself to a major cleaning of an unused third-floor classroom to give himself time to think.

How could he help with the set, how could he talk in a civilized way to Emily, when he was so angry with her?

Maybe Stan would be willing to take over working on the set this time; the man was handy and liked Emily. Probably a little too much.

He was dimly aware that he, himself, was not living up to his responsibilities. What lesson would he give Landon by quitting the show?

His cell rang, and when he looked at it, he saw his boss's name. Of course, he answered right away. "Hey, Ashley. I'm on the third floor. What's up?"

"Is Landon with you?" she asked.

He straightened and gripped the phone tighter. "No, he should be in class."

"He's not," she said. "A couple of the kids said they saw him leave the building."

Dev blew out a sigh. *Cutting school again, Landon? Really?* It was another throwback to his behavior problems back in Denver. "Thanks for letting me know," he said and started putting his supplies away. Deliberately moving slowly, giving himself time to calm down. "I'll find him."

"Hey, Dev…" Ashley said and paused.

"Yeah?" Was there more?

"Just…don't be too hard on him, when you find him. Kids' progress isn't all in one direction. Give him some grace, okay?"

Grace. Not his strongest suit. "I'll try," he said. "Thanks." And he ended the call and started the hunt to find his unhappy, acting-out son.

Chapter Fifteen

At ten o'clock Monday morning, Emily headed into her biweekly meeting with Ashley.

She was dragging, puffy-eyed, but work was the best cure. The meeting happened during her free period, and that was good. The last thing she needed was free, unstructured time. She'd never be able to concentrate on lesson plans or test evaluations, not the way she felt right now.

She'd gotten a double blow on Saturday, with her in-laws' accusations and cruelty and then Dev's rejection. The rest of that day, she'd barely held herself together.

But years of working on her anxiety had shown her how to avoid being debilitated by it.

Sunday, she'd gotten up, taken a long run and then gone to church. She'd forced herself to stay for Sunday school afterward and scored an emergency counseling session with the pastor. She'd gone directly home then, not looking toward Dev's place, and had driven her car—repaired, but still old and loud—to see her mom.

Now, she almost wished she hadn't gone forward with the car repair. She'd lost her tutoring job, and money was again going to be a struggle.

But she'd also lost her ride to visit Mom. How quickly she'd come to depend on Dev's support and Landon's cuteness to get her through her days.

She'd tried to focus on the pastor's words, tried to trust in God. She'd repeated positive Bible verses to herself all the way to and from Mom's care home.

It had helped. She still felt devastated, and she'd still tossed and turned—and cried some—last night. But today she'd gotten up at her regular time, used the hour she should have been tutoring Landon to take another long run with Lady and then gone to work.

She hadn't let herself focus on what her in-laws had said. It was a well-trodden path, although they'd come up with some new twists and turns. She'd think it through sometime, but not now. She knew herself well enough to understand that diving deeply into the past could devastate her, make her unable to do the job she loved, unable to help the children.

Lady stood close as Emily tapped on Ashley's half-open door. "You ready for me?"

"Sure, come on in." Ashley turned from the desktop computer she'd been typing on, smiled and then did a double take. She leaned forward and studied Emily's face, her expression concerned. "Are you okay?"

"I'm fine." She thought about Dev and Ashley coming out of this very office, laughing together.

Ashley didn't have a horrible sin on her conscience, didn't have a tragedy in her past. Ashley was upbeat and professionally successful. And pretty. She'd be a much better match for a man like Dev.

The idea seemed to be at the top of his mind, too. He'd immediately mentioned Ashley as a possible tutoring substitute for Emily.

"You sure?" Ashley gestured for her to sit down, then leaned forward, her face concerned. "Dev told me you're not going to be tutoring Landon anymore."

The words hit Emily like blows. Dev had already confided in Ashley about what had happened. "Did he say why?" she asked, her voice hoarse.

Lady leaned against her and whined, and Emily rubbed the dog's side.

Ashley shook her head. "He just asked if I could help him find another tutor."

That was a small blessing, at least—he hadn't gone into the whole ugly story of what Emily had done.

"I know you've needed the money for your mom's care," Ashley said, her voice kind. "If I hear about any other tutoring options that fit your skills, I'll get in touch right away. You're such a wonderful teacher."

Emily swallowed and stared at a spot on the worn rug. Ashley's kindness was harder to bear than outright cruelty would have been.

And Ashley was right about one thing: Emily was a good teacher. She'd really been helping Landon. He'd liked her, and that was important. He'd looked forward to her tutoring sessions, and it wasn't just about Lady's fun presence; she'd tried to make the lessons relevant to his interests, and he'd responded well.

To substitute another student for Landon... no. She'd looked forward to seeing him. She'd let it get personal, let herself take care of him. Let herself care for him. He was a great kid.

Of course, she'd have to take any other job that came around, whether tutoring or something else. In a small community, there weren't a lot of options. When she'd seen her mother yesterday, Mom had been having a good day, laughing with the staff, smiling at Emily, recognizing her.

Emily needed to keep her mom where she was, safe and as happy as she could be. She blew out a sigh and met Ashley's eyes.

"I know I'm technically your boss, but I'm here as a friend if you need one," Ashley said. "But I won't push you. I'm a private person myself."

Ashley's eyes were steady and kind. Ashley was actually a little younger than Emily, but something in her demeanor had always suggested to Emily that the woman had a lot of life experience.

"Dev dumped me from tutoring Landon," she blurted out. "It wasn't my choice. I would never have left Landon in the lurch."

Ashley nodded. "I didn't think so."

"My, uh, my former in-laws came over and raked me over the coals, pretty loudly, and Dev heard something he didn't like about my past."

Ashley frowned. "Are you willing to share what it was?"

Was she? Could she tell the perfect Ashley what she'd done?

She couldn't feel any worse, any more a pariah, than she did right now. "You've seen my burns," she said, holding out her arm.

Ashley nodded.

"They're from a fire that happened when I'd gone out with friends." She swallowed. "I left my two-year-old home with my husband. He wasn't that reliable, he drank a lot, so I asked my mom to come over and help."

"But your mom has—" Ashley broke off, studying Emily's face.

"Alzheimer's," Emily said. "We didn't know it at the time. Her symptoms were just starting to show, and I never would have thought a woman in her fifties...and Mom loved her grandson so much... Well." She cleared her tight throat. Among the sadness of losing her husband and child, there was grief about Mom, the constant, ongoing loss of the woman she'd been. And *for* Mom, who'd lost everything.

"Anyway," she went on, "Mitch, my husband, fell asleep with the baby. And Mom put a pan on the stove, and then she fell asleep, too. It was an old place, and we didn't have the working smoke detectors I'd thought we did. The fire started up fast, and..." She had to pause, collect herself. "Mitch and the baby died from smoke inhalation. Mom was downstairs, so I was able to pull her out."

The night came back to her in vivid detail. She'd called 911 the moment she'd realized it was her house that was on fire, of course, and the volunteer fire department had responded quickly. The dispatcher had told her to stay away from the house, that they'd have ladders to get safely upstairs, but she'd gone in anyway to find her mother wandering downstairs, disoriented.

She'd tried to fight her way to the stairs, but she hadn't been able to get through the flames. She'd pulled Mom out just as the fire trucks had arrived, and she'd screamed at them that her baby was upstairs. They'd put a ladder to the window she'd indicated and gone up, and they'd come out carrying James, and she'd sagged with relief.

Until she'd noticed the faces of the firemen, which hadn't brightened as they'd carried Mitch out. Though they'd rushed James and Mitch to the hospital, there had been nothing they could do. The lung damage was too great, and they'd both died.

She told Ashley the short version of the story, keeping her voice matter-of-fact while her heart screamed at the telling.

After finishing the story, she looked at Ashley, expecting horror. But instead, the woman's mouth twisted in sympathy. "So…is that really all your fault? Objectively?"

"My in-laws think so. And Dev does, too."

She waved an impatient hand. "What does Dev know? He wasn't there. He heard what your in-laws said, and did he hear any other side of the story? Like yours?"

"My side is the same. It was my fault."

"Really, Emily? Deep in your heart, do you believe you're at fault? Think a minute."

Emily opened her mouth to respond and then shut it again. She thought about what had happened. Had she known Mitch was unreliable? Yes, but she'd tried to cover for that. Had she known her mother had the beginnings of Alzheimer's? Definitely not.

"If I hadn't gone out that night," she said slowly, "they'd still be here."

Ashley nodded, looking sympathetic. "Awful things happen," she said. "But do you mean you should never have gone out? That you should have stayed home with your son every single minute? Was that even possible?"

"No, but—"

"You needed to have friends, have a life, keep perspective. What kind of a mother would you have been if you'd never left the house?"

Ashley's words brought Emily a memory she had forgotten. She'd stayed home with two-year-old James almost all the time she wasn't working, and the strain of it had worn on her. Finally, she'd recognized that she was getting irritable with James and downright angry with Mitch. She wasn't being a good mother or a good wife.

She'd realized how much she missed her friends, how much she needed to get together with them. "I shouldn't have needed to go out. I should have been content with what I had. I didn't know it could be ripped away!" Tears pushed at her eyes, and she blinked, rapidly and hard.

Ashley handed her a box of tissues and then picked up a fancy pen, tapped it on the desk, turned it over, tapped again. "Everyone needs an escape sometimes. Even God rested on the seventh day. You had a two-year-old and worked full-time, right? And a husband who drank? That's a lot."

Emily blew out a sigh. "Yeah. It was." She'd spent so much of the past six years rehashing that one awful night and feeling guilty about it. She hadn't given much thought to the way she'd felt before that, but Ashley's questions were bringing it back to her.

"You tried to take care of yourself, and it backfired in the most horrible way imaginable. That's awful. But does it mean you can't ever take care of yourself again?"

"What do you mean? I run, I eat right—"

"I mean fun. Doing things with friends. Falling in love."

Emily lifted a hand. "Stop. I'm not going there."

But Ashley *didn't* stop. "I've seen how hard you work. How your main recreation is volunteering in town or doing extra jobs at the school. You're very hard on yourself, but you know what? Even that won't keep disaster away. And it won't erase the awful thing that happened to you." She held Emily's eyes steadily. "Through no fault of your own. Understand me? Something awful happened to you, and it wasn't your fault."

The strong statement from a woman she respected opened up a chink in the prison walls Emily had created around herself. A tiny ray of light came in.

"What would God think of what happened? Would He condemn you forever?"

Emily's eyes widened. "No, of course not, because Jesus died for our sins."

Ashley smiled as if Emily were a precocious student. "Exactly."

They sat for a moment, and Emily felt the chink in the walls widen, letting in a little more light.

"I'm disappointed in Dev," Ashley said. "I'm disappointed that he believed your in-laws without finding out the whole story from you."

"I'm disappointed, too," Emily said, surprising herself. "I thought—" She broke off, then studied Ashley's face. "Are you and Dev getting together?"

Ashley looked baffled. And then she laughed. "Oh, because you've seen us together? No, not at all. He's not my type, although I do like him as a friend. And as a friend of both of you, I'm a little mad at him for how he's acting toward you."

Ashley's affirmation brought out something positive in Emily, too. She felt good that Ashley considered her a friend. And she felt *really* thankful that Ashley wasn't dating Dev.

"There's something going on between the two of you, isn't there?" Ashley asked shrewdly. "And don't feel you have to answer that. It's not my business. It's just, I do have eyes."

Emily looked around the office, out the window at the sunny mountain morning. Lady had settled down to sleep beside her. "I can tell you about it," she said, "if you have an hour or so."

Dev was hot and annoyed. He'd be tempted to ground Landon for a year when he found him. For Landon to feel cranky and upset was one thing, that happened to everyone, but skipping school because of it was unacceptable.

He'd looked everywhere he could think of at the school and in its surrounding environment.

He still hadn't found Landon, and now his annoyance was laced with worry.

He covered the ground to the cabin in record time and marched inside. "Landon!"

No answer.

"Landon!" His heart pounded as he strode from room to room.

No sign of his son, but there was a sheet of paper on Landon's bed. Big, angry crayon letters covered the page.

Dev studied it, turned it sideways, tried to decipher it. Clearly, it was a note, an effort at communication. But whether it was because of his worry or Landon's poor handwriting—combined with Dev's newly discovered probable dyslexia—the letters just seemed to jump and blur together.

He jammed it into his pocket and took off running. As he sprinted by Emily's cabin, he called out—"Landon! Hey, Landon!"—but there was neither sight nor sound of his son.

He ran back down toward the school, his work boots pounding, swiveling his head from right to left to search. So many places a boy could be.

With no success, he burst into the school office. "I need to see Ashley," he told Mrs. Henry and strode past her toward the principal's door.

"But she's—"

He ignored the mild protest, knocked and then walked in. And saw Emily sitting in front of Ashley's desk.

Emotions exploded inside him, but there was no time.

"Dev! Emily and I are having a meeting. Is everything okay?"

"I don't know," he said, pulling the paper from his pocket and handing it to Ashley. He couldn't help the feeling of shame that washed over him, but his son was more important than his ego. "Landon's missing, and he left a note. And I can't read it."

Chapter Sixteen

"Landon's missing?" Emily jerked herself out of the comforting warmth of her conversation with Ashley. Swept right past Dev's odd declaration that he couldn't read Landon's note. "For how long? Where'd you see him last?"

"Listen." Ashley was studying the note. "It says he wants Ms. Carver to tutor him. He loves her."

Emily's chest warmed. She loved Landon, too. But where was he?

"And he wants to… Let's see. I think it says he wants to help her." She looked up, then passed the note to Emily. "See what you think—you're more familiar with his writing."

Emily studied the crayon letters. Landon had come a long way with writing in just a few weeks. The spelling was phonetic, but that was a stage. It was easily readable. "He, yes, he wants to help me."

"That's it?" Dev sounded stunned. "No clue about where or how?"

Ashley shook her head and moved over to stand beside Emily so they could both study the note. "You saw that he drew a picture of Lady, and books, right? And…is that money?" She pointed at a couple of rectangles on the page.

Emily looked more closely at the drawings. "Yes. I think those are dollar bills. Look, each picture is labeled. *Dog, bok, mune.* Dog, book, money."

"We need to split up," Ashley said. "Where are the most likely places? I'll get Mrs. Henry to help, but we'll give it ten, fifteen minutes before we call the whole staff into action. If he's just hiding, we don't want to bring attention to that, for his sake and to avoid giving the other boys ideas."

"Makes sense." Dev sounded relieved, and Emily felt that way, too. Ashley took the boys' misbehavior in stride. That was why she was a good administrator of a school like Bright Tomorrows.

Underneath Emily's worry about Landon, hope bloomed in her, a fragile flower. Could Landon's shenanigans repair the rift between her and Dev?

But she shouldn't hope for that. A stronger woman would brush her hands together and move on from a man who'd misjudged her so severely, disappointed her so deeply.

Not Emily, though. Yes, she was strong emotionally, strong enough to rebuild her life after a horrible tragedy, but she was weak inside when it came to love. Dev and Landon had opened her heart when she hadn't thought that could ever happen again.

"I need to stay in the school, so I'll take the library and his classrooms. Because he drew books." Ashley was already turning toward the door. "Dev, I hate to say it, but check anywhere Landon knows there's money. Including the petty cash, if he's ever heard you talk about it, and the cash register we use for guests in the cafeteria."

"And the teachers' lounge, in case people have their wallets there," Dev said grimly. "He's never stolen before, that I know of. But if he took the trouble to write and draw money, that could be what he's up to."

"That covers books and money. Emily, figure out what places he associates with Lady and check those out."

"My cabin and yard, I guess," she said, and turned to Dev. "Did you look there?"

"I went through my cabin, but not yours. I

didn't see him when I ran past, though." His eyes were dark, hooded, but she knew him well enough to see the emotion underneath. Worry about his son, something more complicated about her. And of course, like a man, he was holding it all inside.

"We'll stay in touch by cell and meet back here in fifteen minutes," he said curtly. "Let's go."

Emily read the fear in his eyes. "We'll find him," she said, but he just gave her an unreadable look and didn't speak. Then they all headed in their separate directions.

Emily was glad she'd been running so much as she jogged toward her cabin, pushing her pace as fast as she could in her work shoes, Lady trotting beside her. Her stomach churned with worry about Landon. Surely he was just hiding, though. It had happened with several other boys at the school—efforts to escape punishment, trouble or their own emotions. Because of the school's open layout, every such case had been resolved in a short time, and successfully.

As she got closer to the cabins she smelled something strange—smoke, but an oily, chemical kind of smoke. Familiar panic rose in her, and she put her hand down to touch Lady's head. Someone was burning something nearby.

She turned toward her cabin, Lady beside her,

and stopped, her heart rate shooting up until her whole chest seemed to rattle, nearly choking her.

Was that fire, shooting from the open door of her car?

Panic rose in her, and she ran faster than she'd ever run in her life. "Landon! Landon!" He couldn't be inside the car, with it on fire. Could he? Was he conscious? Like a nightmare, her past pushed into her mind. Thinking the fire was small, contained; going inside to see that it was actually raging through the house. Hoping her family had fled to the neighbors'; figuring the firefighters could save anyone who hadn't made it out.

And learning just how quickly smoke inhalation could kill a strong man and a healthy toddler. "Landon!" she screamed as she got close enough to feel the heat of the blaze, to nearly choke on the oily fumes.

She heard his voice—from outside, not inside the car, sweet relief—but he sounded panicky. The smoke was thick, heavy, awful-smelling. "Landon, come over here, come toward your house." She coughed as she scanned the area with burning, watery eyes. She couldn't see him. This situation was getting more dangerous every minute the fire burned higher. "Get away from the car! Fast!"

Her phone. She tapped the contact number for Dev. "He's at my house and there's a fire!"

She shoved the phone back in her pocket and ran forward, gagging as the oily smoke seemed to coat her throat and nostrils. Heat surged from the car, and the flames grew higher. "Landon! Where are you? Talk to me, yell to me!"

Lady was beside her, and she heard the dog coughing and choking. "Go back," she ordered, pointing, and then went forward herself. "Landon!"

"I can't put it out!" Landon's voice rose in a wail, and she'd never been gladder to hear anything. She followed the sound, and there he was, by the side of the house where she kept her hose, shooting a weak stream of water at the car.

She pulled him into her arms. "I'm so glad you're safe! You scared me so much!" Lady barked beside her as if to echo her words. "Now, come on, get away from the car!" He was too heavy to pick up, so she pulled at him.

"I hafta put it out or I'll get kicked out of school!"

"No, you don't!" Through her fear and her relief and her memories, the fact that they were still in urgent danger was dawning on her. "Come on, we've got to get away."

"No, I hafta put it out!" He struggled out of her arms.

"The car could blow up and hurt us, Landon!" But the panicky boy wouldn't obey.

Dev burst onto the scene, followed by Ashley and Mrs. Henry. "Landon!" Dev picked up Landon with ease. "Come on, get away from the car! Everybody!"

Ashley was pulling at Mrs. Henry, who'd doubled over, probably sickened by the choking smoke. They ran, stumbling and heaving, away from the flaming car.

For a scary moment, Emily couldn't feel Lady beside her. "Lady!" she called, her voice hoarse and ragged. "Lady!" And then she felt the dog's head beneath her hand, heard Lady gagging and choking. Her instinct to protect hadn't allowed her to run as her animal nature surely wanted to do.

Emily grabbed the leash Lady was dragging and started to run, and then there was an explosion. A huge burst of hot air pushed them forward. Emily stumbled, fell, and Lady stopped beside her, nudging at her. Through her confusion and the pain where she'd landed on her knees, she felt an overwhelming determination: no one else was going to be hurt while she had life and breath. She tried to crawl forward, croaking out commands to Lady to go and run, commands the dog disobeyed.

And then Dev was there, picking her up, carrying her out of range of the now wild inferno while she kept a death grip on Lady's leash.

"Come on, let's go!" They all hustled and encouraged each other, choking, all eyes streaming. Emily turned back to see that the car was completely in flames, and way too close to her cabin. Thankfully, she also heard fire trucks.

They reached Landon, and Dev put her down and went to his son. Emily sat, gasping.

Wild, disconnected thoughts swirled. Another fire. Another child at risk. Another connection to her.

Would bad things always follow her?

But this time, at least, no one had been hurt.

Dev made his way back to his cottage, taking Landon with him, and they returned with bottles of water. The five of them—Dev, Landon, Mrs. Henry, Ashley and Emily—sat on the grassy slope and drank water, caught their breath and watched as the firefighters efficiently put out the small blaze.

The rest of the school had heard, of course. Several teachers came out, along with Hayley, and then went back to report to the others. They were a community and they cared.

"What were you doing, Landon?" Emily finally asked, since Dev looked too shaken to say anything.

Landon was crying. "I'm sorry."

"I'm sure you are," Ashley said seriously, "but you know setting a fire is a very dangerous thing. You know you're never supposed to do that."

"It was to help Ms. Carver," he protested. "Remember? Mr. Davidson said it would be better if her car burned up so she could get the 'surance money. And she needed money after Dad said she couldn't tutor me anymore." He rubbed his eyes with dirty fists. "I was just trying to help."

All the adults stared at him.

"Well, if that's not the sweetest thing," Mrs. Henry said.

Ashley shook her head. "It's sweet and foolish. Never again, Landon."

Emily's heart melted, and she hugged Landon. "Thank you," she said, her voice breaking. "The way you did it was very, very wrong, but your heart was pure."

Dev looked over at her. "He almost died. Don't encourage him."

Dev was still taking an attitude toward her, which rankled. But Landon and Lady and everyone were safe. Emily wasn't going to focus on one man's negativity, no matter how much she cared for him. She looked up at the sky and whispered her thanks.

"Daddy, I left you a note. I wrote it myself. So you could find it."

"I…"

"Did you read it? Did you?"

He blew out a breath. "I tried. Ms. Carver and Dr. Green helped."

"'Cause you can't read," Landon said, sighing.

Ashley stood and held out a hand to Landon. "Why don't you come with me," she said. "I think the firefighters will want to talk to you."

Landon's lip started to tremble.

"Daddy?"

"He'll be right behind you. He needs a minute with Ms. Carver." She firmly led Landon away.

Emily stared at Dev. "You know," she said, "I'm not going to care what you think, not anymore. You're blaming me for something that's not a sin. Maybe I used bad judgment to thank him for what he did, but I don't think so, because he's already beating himself up and I'm sure there will be consequences. Meanwhile, he needs to know someone loves him."

She stood. "I'm going to go check on my home. Oh, and Dev," she said. "I thought we were friends, at least. So why didn't you tell me you couldn't read?"

On Wednesday, Dev, Landon and Chip pulled into the church parking lot as soon as school was over.

Play rehearsals had been postponed while Emily recovered—she was the only one of them who'd sustained a few burns, and according to Ashley, her PTSD had kicked up enough that her doctor had ordered her to rest. So they'd come to the church. Landon was happy for the chance to skateboard around the church parking lot while Dev met with his cousin.

Dev was mostly just happy Landon was alive and safe.

They'd both had trouble sleeping the night after the fire. Yesterday had been a day of talking to the fire chief and Ashley, Landon's fearful, shaky apologies, discussions of consequences. They hadn't seen much of Emily; after the school nurse had bandaged her knees and arm, Ashley had driven her to the hospital. She'd been pronounced fine, according to Ashley, just in need of a couple of days off. She seemed to have retreated into her cabin, which thankfully hadn't caught fire nor sustained any water damage.

Dev couldn't think about Emily, not yet. His feelings were too confused. So he focused on Landon. He wanted to figure out what had possessed the boy to take such a radical route to what he wanted, but he also just wanted to keep his son close. Those moments when he'd run toward the burning car, before he'd seen that

Emily had Landon and that both were safe, had been the worst of his life.

It kept flooding his mind: how Emily must have felt, losing her child and husband in a fire.

And shame pushed at him because of how he'd judged her. He realized, now, that he himself could be judged just as harshly. He'd upset Landon, hadn't kept on top of his mental state enough to realize how distressed and desperate he was at the notion of losing Emily as a tutor.

He parked the car, and the boys opened the doors and scrambled out. "Landon." Dev used his most serious voice. "Wait a minute. Chip, you can start skateboarding, just here in the parking lot. Landon will join you in a few minutes."

"Aw, Dad..." Landon broke off when he saw Dev's expression.

"This is about getting you some counseling, first off," he said. "We're going to talk to Uncle Nate about it." That was one part of the agreement that Landon could stay at the school, even after doing something as serious as starting a fire: that he have counseling. And they'd all decided it would be good for him to work with Dev's cousin the pastor, who was trained in doing therapy with young people and who would include a strong spiritual element in the discussions.

"Hey, cousin." Nate came out of the church, his old jeans indicating he was ready to work. Dev had offered to help repair the retaining wall beside the church's outdoor pavilion. "Landon, what's this I hear about you doing something stupid for a very kind reason?"

Landon had to puzzle that one out, but he clearly understood that Nate wasn't angry and wasn't going to take a punishing attitude toward him. He wrinkled his nose and grinned. "I was wrong to set the fire and I know it. And I know I hafta talk to you about it, but do I hafta do it now?"

"Landon," Dev scolded. "Attitude. If Uncle Nate wants to talk to you now, you'll talk to him now."

"But Chip—" Landon glanced longingly toward his friend, who was practicing skateboard passes at the far end of the parking lot. "Yes, sir. Thank you, sir."

Nate smiled. "I think if we set up a half-hour session every Saturday morning, that'll be fine. And we might be able to do it while skateboarding. I'm pretty good at it myself."

Dev laughed. He remembered.

Landon stared. "But you're—" He broke off and looked at Dev.

"I'm old, I know." Nate gave an easy laugh. "I don't take the risks I used to, but I can teach you some tricks. Now, go practice some ollies with your friend. I've got work to do with your dad."

"Thanks!" Landon ran over to Chip, his board under his arm.

Dev scratched his head. "Really, you still skateboard?"

"Good way to reach the kids. How do you think I sprained my wrist last year?"

"Like Landon started to say, you're old."

"Not as old as you, *primo*." Nate slid easily into using the Spanish word for cousin. "Now, let's get to work and you can tell me the real story about what happened up at the school two days ago."

They went to the shed behind the church and found shovels, trowels, premixed cement and a wheelbarrow. Once they'd carried it all to the site where Nate wanted the wall repaired, they started digging out the broken section.

"Since you said you wanted the real story," Dev said, "I assume that means the rumors are flying."

"They are. Ranging from 'those delinquents tried to burn down the school' to 'that McCarthy boy is a real sweetheart' to 'the new handyman committed a crime of passion to get the attention of the reading teacher.'"

That last one had Dev leaning on his shovel. None of it was true, of course, but the idea of passion toward the reading teacher... "Let me tell you what happened," he said.

So he filled Nate in on the incident, beyond the bare details they'd discussed on the phone. Nate whistled. "You could have lost him, man. Her, too. If that car had blown up any sooner..." He shook his head.

"I know. Thinking about losing Landon has made for some sleepless nights." And was continuing to give him empathy over what Emily had gone through. Empathy that had no outlet, because he hadn't seen her since the fire. He'd texted her a couple of times, had tried to call, but she hadn't answered.

"Well. I'm sure you've talked to him about safety and thinking through decisions, and I'll reinforce that in the counseling sessions," Nate said. "Is he at risk of being expelled from the school?"

"Thankfully, no." Dev pulled out a couple of big rocks, welcoming the effort and the strain on his muscles. The newly uncovered ground sent up an earthy, sage-like smell, unique to this part of Colorado, Dev suspected. "The principal is very understanding. She held a staff meeting and talked about what happened, and everyone got behind giving Landon another chance. Only one, though." He shaded his eyes and looked over to where Landon and Chip played, the picture of happy, carefree boyhood. "I don't think he'll do it again. I think he learned his lesson."

"You thought that last time, correct?"

Dev gave a wry grin and carried more rocks to the wheelbarrow. "Yeah. I did."

"So there's going to be prayer involved as well as counseling and discipline. Because none of us can parent kids without the help of the Lord."

"For sure." Dev didn't often pray with Landon, just reminded him to say his prayers. Maybe that needed to change.

It was Nate's turn to lean on his shovel. "Seems like Landon is pretty fond of Miss Emily Carver. Does that hold for you, too?"

Dev glanced over, realized he couldn't minimize it to his astute cousin and nodded. "Yeah. I care."

"Is it serious?"

Dev shook his head and started laying thick, plaster-like cement over the exposed top of the stones. "No," he said, "because I wrecked it."

"How'd you do that?" Nate carried over a couple of rocks and lined them up where Dev had prepared the wall.

Dev sealed the cracks between the stones and didn't look at his cousin. "I was ashamed because I... I really can't read, much. Tried to hide it, and was a jerk toward her." He'd been judgmental toward her without knowing her whole story, just based on what her in-laws had said. That was his biggest mistake, but he didn't want to go into that with Nate. It was Emily's story to tell or keep private.

His reading problems were part of it, though, and he waited for Nate to express shock about them.

Nate kept bringing over rocks. "Uh-huh."

"Wait a minute." Dev put down his trowel and faced his cousin. "You knew I had problems with reading?"

"I did." Nate glanced over. "Knew you couldn't read, and knew you were ashamed about it."

Huh. Nate knew, and Landon had known, too. Obviously, Dev hadn't kept the big deep secret he'd thought he had.

"You didn't look down on me for it?" He couldn't believe that. Not after being called stupid in several of his foster homes and a couple of schools, not after Roxy's belittling of him.

But Nate just frowned like Dev was being an idiot. "Of course I didn't look down on you. For one thing, you're a child of God no matter what your abilities or disabilities. And for another, you're crazy smart."

"I'm crazy smart." Dev stated it flatly, because the idea was so ridiculous. "Right."

"You are! You've always been able to fix everything in sight—without reading the directions, obviously—and you have a memory like an elephant." He snorted. "Not saying you're smart in every area. You're pretty dumb when it comes to women."

"That's for sure." They went on working, and Dev thought about the conversation.

Nate had turned around Dev's worldview with just a few sentences. Really, he was smart? Dev wouldn't go that far, but he did know Nate was right about his mechanical skills. He could look at an array of disassembled parts—whether of a furnace, a car or a Swedish warehouse bookcase—and see, in his head, how it all fit together. He was always surprised when other people couldn't do the same.

His memory was a product of necessity. He'd had to train himself to recall every word of a lecture in high school, every explanation a teacher had made of how to solve a math problem. Same on the job, and it had just carried over into the rest of his life.

That skills like that bespoke intelligence had never occurred to him.

He knew he wasn't book smart—the total opposite, in fact. But maybe that wasn't the only kind of smart.

For a woman like Emily, though, books and

reading were central. And in those areas, Dev was pretty much an imbecile.

Nate had carted off a wheelbarrow load of broken rocks and dirt, and now he came back across the yard with a load of new, rounded stones. As he started laying them atop the cement Dev had troweled on, he spoke. "Truth is," he said, "I don't think your problems with women—with Emily in particular—have to do with literacy at all."

"What do you mean?" Yeah, he'd been a jerk in other ways, but it all came back to that basic inadequacy in him.

"Reading and writing are important, and I can see why it would be hard to lack skill in those areas," Nate said, starting to sound like the preacher he was. "But those are outward things. I think the real problem is deeper." He turned from his work and tapped his chest. "I think it's your heart."

Here it came, the lecture. Dev spread the last of the cement.

There was something wrong with him, and he'd been told it in so many ways that he'd learned to tune it out.

"In your heart," Nate went on, "you don't believe you're smart and successful enough, *good* enough, to be loved. To have a family.

And to be loved by a smart, beautiful woman like Emily—"

Dev went on alert and glared at his cousin. "Wait a minute, you think she's smart and beautiful? What, are you hitting on her?"

"Nope." Nate grinned. "Not that it didn't occur to me, when I first met her. I'm a single guy her age, and she's a great woman. But I could tell she didn't feel a spark. I'm not one to chase after someone who doesn't want me, so I turned my attention elsewhere."

"Good. Keep it there."

"You're creating a distraction from my point," Nate said patiently, as if Dev were a recalcitrant parishioner. "The way you've closed off your heart from love and a family makes sense, given the way you grew up."

"I've gotten over all that." Dev had gone through periods of resentment about the families who'd passed him off to someone else, as an adolescent, but he'd come to peace with it. "I know it's hard for foster parents. Most of them aren't in it to raise a child all the way to adulthood. And I was a handful."

Nate snickered. "You were. But then, so was I. So are most boys." He nodded toward Landon. "Ever think about giving him up? Passing him back off to Roxy? He set a fire, after all."

Dev stared at Nate. "No way!"

"Exactly. And that's how my parents felt when I stole from the corner drugstore and cheated on a math exam. They were angry, they punished me, I learned. But nobody ever thought about giving me away."

Giving him away. No, Nate's parents wouldn't have given him away, any more than Dev would give Landon away.

"You've reconciled what happened in your head, I'm sure," Nate went on. "But your heart knows it wasn't fair, and maybe your heart doesn't want to risk opening up to that kind of hurt again."

This was getting a little too heavy for Dev. "Thanks. I'll think about what you said." He brushed the dirt off his hands and turned away.

"Just don't let it stop here," Nate called after him. "Don't let it define you."

Dev thought about what a jerk he'd been to Emily. He stopped walking, turned back. "I think I already did." Because he'd pushed her away well and hard.

Nate's gaze was steady. "You giving up? He didn't." Nate pointed toward Landon.

Dev looked at his son, still running and playing, cheeks red, arms and legs pumping, laughter flowing out of his mouth.

Nate was right. Landon had screwed up, both in school and in his behavior. But he wasn't turning into a sullen failure. He'd picked himself up, apologized, worked hard. And he was ready to try again.

Could Dev do any less? "I don't want to give up," he said, "but I really did ruin things with Emily."

"Like I said," Nate said, "you're pretty smart. You can find a way to fix it."

Dev frowned after him, thinking. How did you fix something like what he'd done to Emily?

It couldn't be some quick apology, something that didn't seem sincere. It had to be bigger. And not just six bouquets of roses or a bunch of balloons like you saw on the feel-good shows he and Landon liked to watch in the mornings, while they had breakfast and got ready for the day.

No, for Emily, he needed to do something meaningful.

He stared at the wall they'd repaired, thinking, and it came to him. He knew exactly what he needed to do. "You might have to help me."

"We need water," Chip gasped out in mock drama beside him.

"Help me apologize to Ms. Carver for some things I said and did," Dev admitted.

"Oh, sure, I'll help," Landon said.

Dev wanted to grab his son in his arms and hug him. For being safe, for being helpful, for being an inspiration. But they were guys, so instead, he just pointed at the hose. "Water's over there," he said, and laughed as they ran to soak themselves, not accidentally, while they drank deeply from it.

Chapter Seventeen

The Sunday after the fire, Emily sat beside her mother at the little table in her room. An aide had opened a window, and the warm breeze from outside carried with it the smells of pine and sage, the trills and whistles of birds that gathered at the feeders outside. She, Hayley and Ashley had driven here together in Ashley's car, and Emily's friends had gone shopping while she visited her mother. Afterward, they were all going to a concert.

Mom seemed peaceful today. A new exercise routine had done wonders for her mood, according to her caregivers. They'd gotten her to join a group that walked for fifteen to thirty minutes daily, and she'd started doing a gentle strength-training class twice a week. That, combined with an experimental new medication, seemed to be having a good effect. Mom looked almost like she'd used to look, rosy cheeked, her face unlined.

It inspired Emily. "Hey, Mom, I need to talk to you."

"Sure, what's the latest?" It was a phrase Mom had used during their discussions before the diagnosis, and Emily's throat tightened.

She leaned closer to the bed and took her mother's hand, holding it lightly. "I think I kind of messed up," she said. "I thought I had a, well, a relationship, but it didn't work out."

"The man who comes?" Mom asked.

"Yes."

"I like him," Mom declared. "He has good hair like your father did."

That made Emily smile. Her father had had thick, curly hair. She thought of Dev's hair, how it had felt beneath her hands. "Yes, he does."

"Why are you giving him up?" Mom asked.

"He judged me harshly."

"For the fire?"

Emily tensed. Mom usually got upset when the subject of fire came up. But since she'd gone in that direction mentally, there was no point in trying to turn her back. "Yes. He thinks the fire was my fault."

"It was *my* fault." Mom frowned.

"It was all of our faults." Emily took her hand,

her stomach twisting. *Please, Mom, don't freak out now.*

But her mother met her eyes in much the way she'd used to. "I'm sorry," she said simply. "Sometimes, all you can say is I'm sorry. Do you forgive me?"

"Of course I forgive you!" Emily leaned forward and gave her mother a careful hug. "I forgive you for what role you played, if you'll forgive me for what role I played. We both lost so much."

"Ye-es…" Mom looked confused and began to twist her hands. She'd forgotten the subject of their conversation.

Emily went over to the shelf of family picture albums, took one down, and brought it back to her mother's bedside. They'd never looked through it before, because Emily feared it would upset her mother. In fact, Emily had never looked through it herself; it was an album Mom had made, back when she'd been healthy and into scrapbooking.

But today just might be the day.

She pulled her chair close beside her mother's and opened the album.

The pictures took her rushing back to the past. There was the sonogram, and a photo of herself pregnant. There was James as a newborn, so red-faced and wrinkly.

Oh, how she'd loved him. Loved being a mother.

Mom turned the page and pointed to a photo of herself, holding James, who couldn't have been more than two days old. "Sweet baby," she said.

Emily nodded, blinking back tears. "He was. He really was."

Slowly, they paged forward, looking at the milestones: first smile, first tooth, scooting, sitting up, crawling, walking. Emily was in some of the pictures, Mitch in some, Mom in others. Those had been such good days.

Oh, she hadn't always been happy at those times. She and Mitch had struggled; the partying lifestyle that hadn't bothered her before James's birth had gotten worrisome afterward. She hadn't communicated her feelings well. She was pretty sure she'd nagged him into sneaking around, spending money they didn't have, taking up with a rougher group of friends.

But, as evidenced by the photos, they'd had some good moments. They'd both loved their son.

Mom had, too.

Emily blew her nose and looked at Mom, who was smiling, running a finger over a big studio picture of James at age one. "He's in Heaven," she said. "I'll see him there, soon."

Emily blinked. "Oh, no, Mom. Not for a long time."

"I'm ready to go."

"No, Mom!" As far as Emily knew, it was possible Mom would live another twenty years. She wasn't even sixty yet. On the other hand, Alzheimer's was a killer. Today, it seemed like Mom knew that.

"When the time comes," she said, "I'll take care of little James for you. And in Heaven, I'll do it perfectly, with no mistakes."

Emily's eyes filled with tears again. "Oh, Mom," she said. "I don't want you to go, but I'm glad you'll take care of him. I know you'll be wonderful at it."

And until that time came, Emily resolved, she'd make sure Mom had all the care and love it was possible for her to have. Today had reminded her that Mom was still here, even behind the curtain of her disease.

Of course, every day wouldn't be this good. Mom was likely to swing back into confusion and distress soon, and Emily knew the proportion of bad days would increase, maybe slowly, maybe quickly.

She could hope that the new regimen would keep Mom with her a little longer. Regardless, Emily would love her and do her best to make sure she could stay here, receiving good care.

Which meant, of course, that she needed to find another job so that she didn't slip back into the money problems she'd had before starting to tutor Landon.

It took most of the concert before Emily had recovered enough from her emotional day with her mother to get into the music.

When she did, she was glad she'd come.

Christine Deschamps was a Christian singer who'd gone back and forth from performing to not performing, whose struggles with a stalker and ultimate happy marriage to her bodyguard had been big in the news. When she sang, it was as if you could hear all that history in her voice and in her music, most of which she'd composed herself. She was beautiful, and talented, and wildly popular…and Ashley happened to know her. So after the concert, they were able to meet her in her dressing room and share girl talk and faith talk, until her husband and bodyguard, Logan Scott, knocked on the door and suggested she finish up so they could get home. She insisted he come in and meet her friends, old and new. They all left a little bit starstruck.

"That bodyguard-slash-husband was seriously hot," Hayley said on the ride home. "Why don't I ever meet somebody like that?"

"Christine went through some very hard times in order to meet him," Ashley said from the driver's seat. She maneuvered the mountain road skillfully, at a slow pace that was appropriate for the darkness.

"Didn't you think so?" Hayley asked Emily, turning around from the passenger seat. Emily had insisted on taking the back seat, because she'd been grateful that they had driven her to her mother's place. And maybe a little so that she could keep it to herself if she got emotional.

She felt scraped raw. The past that had come up today, with Mom, and Mom's up-and-down state generally, was a constant presence in the back of her mind. Landon and Dev were another. They'd seen each other during the past week; Dev had made courteous inquiries about her injuries and how she was doing, and she'd checked on Landon. But it had all stayed at a distant, impersonal level after the huge, heavy emotions of the fire.

The fact that Dev couldn't read, or not well, had shocked her at first. He was so *good* at things, it was hard to imagine he had such a major deficit.

And it was hurtful that he hadn't seen fit to tell her, when they'd talked so much about Landon's literacy needs. You'd think it would have come up. Didn't he trust her?

But in the days since, she'd thought more about it and even gone back to one of her old textbooks that talked about adult illiteracy, something she hadn't studied nearly as much as children's issues with reading. It was a more common problem than most people realized, simply because a lot of adults found ways to work around it. Also, it was embarrassing to many who struggled. Expecting Dev to be open about it was probably asking too much.

That part she could understand. But he'd also put her down, thought the worst of her, blamed her. He'd placed himself squarely in her in-laws' camp, and now she felt like she couldn't trust him.

"Well, didn't you?" Hayley persisted from the front seat.

"Didn't I what?" Emily needed to get out of her own head and pay attention to her friends.

"Didn't you think Christine's husband, Logan, was hot?"

"Truthfully? I barely noticed him. I'm a little distracted." She meant by her day with her mother.

But Hayley narrowed her eyes. "By Dev? I can't think of any other reason you'd barely notice that amazing specimen of manhood."

"Stop objectifying Logan," Ashley said. "He's

a smart guy who walks the talk of his faith. And he treats Christine like a queen."

"Okay, okay, sorry." Hayley raised a hand. "My bad. Emily. Tell us what's distracting you and making you so quiet back there."

"Well, it's a little bit about Dev. Maybe more than a little," she said. "But it's also about my mom. Since I've lost the tutoring job, I'm going to have to find a way to keep paying the bills."

"Are you sure you've lost the tutoring job? Did you talk to Dev about it?" Ashley glanced over her shoulder. "I'm pretty sure he'd re-hire you. You were doing so much good with Landon."

"I miss him," she admitted. "But the thing is, I was getting too attached and so was he."

"You're not too attached," Hayley said, "if you and Dev get together. Then, it'll be good if you're attached to his son."

"Yeah." Emily swallowed. "But that's not happening. And the truth is, I have an interview for another job."

Ashley braked and glanced back over her shoulder. "You *what*?"

She sighed. "I might as well tell you. It's an hour in the other direction from Mom's place. It's a private school, and it pays more, enough that I could keep Mom in her care home easily. I don't want to go, don't get me wrong. But…

there are reasons it would be good for me to leave in addition to the one we've talked about, Landon getting too close."

"Reasons like what?" Hayley sounded like she was about to cry. "I can't handle it if you go."

"I know. I'm still thinking about it. I value my friends at Bright Tomorrows, so much. But the truth is..." She paused.

To their credit, like the good friends they were, Ashley and Hayley didn't rush her.

"The truth is, I don't think I can stay here and watch Dev and Landon from afar. I care. Too much, and not just as a friendly colleague or a tutor."

"Are you sure it's not about money?" Ashley asked. "Because we could work on a little bit of a raise..."

"And Pastor Nate has a potential job at the church, helping interpret for the Spanish-speaking community. I'm sure you could get it."

She shook her head. "You're both sweet, but it's not about that, as much as the other. That I can't..." Her throat tightened too much to speak as the possible future formulated before her.

Dev waving, unsmiling, as he'd done for the last week. Landon moving on with another tutor.

Dev moving on with another woman.

"It's okay." Hayley reached back and patted

her leg, and Ashley turned up the radio, and Emily had the time to collect herself.

When Emily got dropped off at her place, she hurried inside, wanting Lady. She'd gone out on a limb and asked if Landon could feed her and let her out, for pay, checking with Dev first. By impersonal text, and he'd responded equally impersonally that it was fine, the responsibility and the chance to earn a little money would be good for Landon.

That was what she had to look forward to, she thought as she lct Lady out and then ushered her back inside. She sat down on the couch, and Lady jumped up beside her, seeming to know that Emily needed comfort.

She and Dev would be impersonal friends, colleagues. Maybe she'd give Landon a hand from time to time. Maybe she'd refocus on re-building her life as a single person. She could go on some of those women's trips Hayley was always asking her to go on. She could go out at night. Go out with someone who wasn't Dev.

She rested her face on Lady's sturdy side. "I just don't want that," she murmured to the dog.

Something brushed against her face. She looked and noticed, for the first time, that there was a plastic bag attached to Lady's collar with twist ties.

She pulled it free and looked inside.

She smiled a little. This looked like Landon's work. She opened the plastic bag and drew out the paper.

A letter. But it wasn't from Landon. She started to read.

Early the next morning, Dev paced in his kitchen, looking over at Emily's house.

Had she gotten the letter? Had she read it?

Had she despised it? Laughed at it?

It was six thirty. In half an hour, Landon would be up and wanting breakfast. And then Landon would have to go to school, and Dev to work. And he wouldn't know how Emily had reacted.

Now or never. He gathered his courage, strode across the two yards and knocked on Emily's door.

She opened it immediately, a cup of coffee in her hand. She didn't say a word, although her eyes were wide with some kind of emotion he couldn't interpret.

And then he saw that the letter was in her other hand.

"Did you—could you—read it?" he asked, stumbling over his words. His heart hammered like a drum.

She nodded. "Of course I did. Of course I could. Thank you."

"You're welcome." He stood then, looking at her. Wasn't she going to react any more than that?

Of course, maybe it wasn't a big deal to her. After all, she wrote letters all the time.

Or maybe she'd been shocked at how rudimentary was his spelling, his handwriting, his style. "I didn't have anyone check it," he stammered. "I just, I didn't want anyone else but you to read it. I warned Landon before he put it on Lady's collar that he wasn't to try to read it." He held his breath.

She came out onto the porch, put her arms around his neck and kissed his cheek. "It was a beautiful letter, Dev. I appreciate the apology, and I would never judge you for what's probably a reading disability, and which is definitely not your fault."

"I should have known that," he said. "I know your kindness. I know you don't make fun of people or look down on them. I should have trusted you more."

She smiled at him. "Yes, you should have."

But she wasn't softening the way he'd hoped she would. Maybe because he hadn't been able to say all he felt in that letter he'd labored over for hours. "Can we sit down a minute?"

She looked back toward her kitchen. "Um, sure." She was dressed for work, in a blue-and-white-striped dress, tied at her slender waist, flowy around her legs. She sat on the top step and tucked her legs under her.

"Look," he said, "I'm not the most articulate guy, and definitely not on paper. I wanted you to see that I trust you now, but…there's more to say."

"Yeah?" She snapped her fingers, and Lady came to her side and leaned against her.

She needed emotional support to be around Dev. Well, he'd earned that. He'd been awful to her. And while his apology might have helped, she still didn't quite trust him, and understandably so.

He sucked in a breath and prepared to make the speech of his life. "Emily, I just want you to know that I think you're an incredible woman. You're beautiful, but that's not it. You're kind and good." He needed to show her the words weren't just empty, and that was easy to do, because the examples crowded into his mind. "You're wonderful with the kids, and you've helped me and Landon feel at home here. You volunteer at the church and in the community, but you always have time for your friends. And you're smart, smarter than I'll ever be."

Finally, she cracked a smile. "Well, smart at

books. I'm not smart at repairing a car or building a stage set."

"But see, that's why we'd make a good team," he said. "You're good at some things, and I'm good at others, and we could help each other become better. Or just do things for each other. I'd fix your car anytime."

Two vertical creases formed between her eyebrows. "What are you suggesting? A business partnership?"

Lord, show me how to do this better. He took her hand and squeezed it, gently. "No. I'm proposing we get to know each other better."

Her eyes widened. "You mean like dating?"

"Like dating. I would love to take you out to the movies, or a nice dinner. Or on a romantic picnic." Yeah, he'd love that a lot. "I'd like to give you the chance to get to know me better, and then maybe, if you did…"

The front door of his cabin opened. Landon came out, spotted them and ran over at top speed. "Did you ask her?"

"Ask her what, son?" He put an arm around Landon, who'd gotten dressed but clearly hadn't washed his face, combed his hair or brushed his teeth yet. The kid was a mess.

"To marry you!"

Dev's jaw nearly dropped. He stole a glance

at Emily. She looked shocked, too. Her cheeks were pink.

"Landon, I wasn't—"

"It's okay with me. I want you to marry her, and she could be like my mom…" He frowned, obviously thinking it through, while Dev tried to figure out how to stop this premature, kid-created marriage proposal. "Like my second mom, and Lady could be partly my dog." He ducked out from under Dev's arm and moved over to Lady, putting both arms around her.

Lady licked his face.

Dev's own face felt hot. Should he backtrack, back off, deny what his son had said?

But from somewhere in his heart, he found the courage and strength to seize the opportunity. He turned toward Emily and took her hand. "Look, Landon kind of jumped the gun. I didn't intend to say that today, to propose, but it's what I had in mind."

She looked skeptical. "Really, Dev?"

Tell the truth. You don't have to hide your real self from her. "Really. Hey, Landon, why don't you take Lady over to our yard and run around with her for a few?"

"Yeah!" Landon jumped up, then looked at Emily. "Is that okay?"

"Um, I guess?" She brushed her hands through her hair as Landon and Lady took off.

Game time. Dev got on one knee, his heart pounding. "Emily, I do want to marry you. Nothing would make me happier, because you're the best woman I've ever known, and when you smile, it's like the sunrise." He sucked in a breath.

She bit her lip, her mood unreadable.

He'd started, so he needed to finish. "I know this is way too fast and I have a lot to prove. I was so quick to judge you, and I'm not... Well." He looked down, then back into her eyes. "I wasn't going to ask you until I'd gotten better at reading," he said. "Someone like you, so smart, such a book person, I know you couldn't consider—"

"Dev. Wait." Her voice sounded a little shaky, and she squeezed his hand and dropped it. "Please don't tell me all the things that are wrong with you, just tell me if you...if you really mean it, what you're saying about how you feel."

He moved up to sit beside her and wrapped one arm around her, gently. "I've never meant anything more," he said. "I love you, Emily."

"You..." She pressed a hand to her mouth. "You're not just saying that?"

"I'm not just saying it, and I'm not just following Landon's lead. Although it matters a lot, how much he cares for you." He drew in a breath and told her what was true. "I'm sincere in wanting to marry you. When you're ready. If you're ever ready. No pressure."

Emily looked into Dev's eyes, so anxious, so warm. Emotions rose in her, and she put a hand over her mouth. "You just asked me to marry you."

Somewhere across the yards, she could hear Lady barking and Landon shouting. Here on the porch, there was only Dev. Handsome, nervous, flawed, wonderful Dev.

"Is there any chance you'll say yes? Not now, but if I can prove to you that I'm a man worthy of marrying? Even though I messed up pretty badly, and I'll probably do it again and again?"

"You're forgiven." And it was true. He'd been wrong to judge her, but he was admitting his mistakes. What more could a woman ask?

"Then you'll think about it?"

She touched his cheek. "I will. You're a wonderful father and a caring man, and… I really care about you." She paused, then let herself say the wonderous truth. "I care about you, and I… yeah. I think, no, I know… I love you."

She felt dazed, renewed, joyous. Thankful. So very thankful.

Dev put a hand on either side of her face. "You just made me so happy. I don't have words for it, except... I'll say it again. I love you, Emily." And then he kissed her.

And she melted into his arms, her heart full. This wonderful man wanted to marry her, and as she searched inside herself, she realized that the last bitter chains around her heart had broken, leaving her free. Free to love. Free to allow herself happiness. Free to reach for joy.

He lifted his head. "I'm so glad you didn't turn me down flat," he said, laughing a little. "Man, when Landon blurted that out... I did plan a better buildup. And I'll do a proper proposal, with a ring, when we've had a chance to really date. I want to show you how well I can treat you, Emily. Not just as a coworker and team player and neighbor, but as a man who's crazy in love with you."

"That sounds wonderful," she said, "and I want you to do it. I *really* want it, so don't think you can get out of it! But Dev." She laid a hand along his clean-shaven cheek. "The truth is, I don't need time. When you pulled me out of that fire, I knew how I felt. So...yes. I love you, and I want to marry you. The sooner, the better."

Dev whooped and picked her up and twirled her in his strong arms. "She said yes!"

And then Landon and Lady were jumping around them both, and Dev kissed her right there in front of them. And then they all hugged, and Stan came out of his cabin to see what all the fuss was about.

And then they went to work, because the world didn't stop just because they'd fallen in love and decided to get married.

It only felt like it had.

Epilogue

∼◆∼

Two months later

"I really don't want to do this." Emily sat in the Mountaineer Café, drinking coffee with Ashley and Hayley, Lady dozing on the floor at their feet. Around them, bridal magazines and books on wedding planning were scattered over the table.

She looked longingly over at Dev and Landon, who sat at a table on the other side of the restaurant with Pastor Nate. Landon was fidgeting, playing with an action figure, nearly knocking over a glass of water. Dev looked almost as fidgety.

She wanted to go over there and hug him. Wanted to be with him and Landon. Even though they'd spent nearly every day since getting engaged together, it wasn't enough. She couldn't wait to start being a real family together.

"If you're getting married, you have to start planning your wedding," Ashley insisted. "That's why we're here, because when we're on campus, you always find other things to do."

"It's our version of an intervention," Hayley said. "If you don't start planning now, the campus is going to combust with all the romance swirling between you and Dev." She clapped her hand to her mouth. "I'm sorry. Fire metaphors are so wrong with you."

Emily patted Hayley's arm. "It's okay," she said. And it was. She'd truly resolved her feelings, with the help of Dev and an assist from Pastor Nate, who'd been doing some premarital counseling with them. "There *is* a lot of romance between us. We can't wait to get married. It's just, neither of us is that interested in this stuff." She waved a hand at the books and magazines.

"Maybe you should just run away together," Hayley suggested.

Ashley clapped her hands. "Not a bad idea. We could stop hounding you about wedding planning."

"That sounds wonderful." Emily propped her cheek on her hand. "But it won't work. Landon has to be involved, and we want a church wedding."

She sighed and looked over at Dev, Nate and Landon. Nate had a laptop out and was looking at Dev with an expression of impatience.

Dev caught her eye and mouthed the word *help!*

"You know," Emily said slowly, "maybe we don't have to run away. Maybe we could just sort of elope right here in town."

Hayley's forehead wrinkled.

But Ashley lifted her hands, palms up. "Why not? Hey, Nate! Dev, Landon, c'm'ere!"

Landon ran over, followed more slowly by the two men.

Dev put a hand on Emily's shoulder and squeezed, and they shared a smile. She felt so much better just being close to him.

"Pull up some chairs," Ashley ordered, showing her leadership skills. "We have a proposition."

Nate raised his eyebrows. "Oh, you do, do you?"

"We do." And quickly Ashley summed up the elopement idea. "I'd suggest doing it today, but I'm sure there are legal details to manage."

Nate looked thoughtful. "Not really. All you have to do is drive over to the county clerk's office. It's pretty relaxed here in Colorado."

"No waiting period?" Dev asked.

Nate shook his head. "No. And no witnesses needed. As a matter of fact, I knew one couple who had their dog sign their marriage license."

Landon's eyes lit up. "Could Lady sign?"

Emily put an arm around him and ruffled his hair. "Only if you sign, too."

"I can do that! I'm good at writing now!"

"You are *so* doing this," Hayley said. "Pastor Nate, I know Mondays are usually your day off, but do you have time to perform a wedding?"

Nate looked at his watch, laughed and nodded. "For my favorite cousin, I think I can fit it in."

"I have a white sundress you can borrow," Ashley said to Emily.

Emily felt breathless in the best possible way. She looked at Dev. "What do you think?"

His forehead wrinkled. "I want you to have the wedding you want. Flowers, bridesmaids, the works."

"The works isn't what I want," she said. "I just want to be married to you. With as little fuss as possible."

His face broke into a huge smile. "I for sure just want to be married to you. As soon as possible. The less fuss, the better." He turned to Nate. "Could we really do it today?"

"If you get in the car with your fiancée and hit the county clerk's office."

"And we'll stay back here and get things ready," Hayley said. She hugged Emily. "This is perfect!"

Emily couldn't have agreed more.

So it was that on Monday, July 21, in their own church, with a few friends, Landon and Lady all sitting in the front pews, Emily and Dev were married.

Afterward, they had dinner at the only restaurant in the area that was open on a Monday. Emily felt joyous, surrounded by her friends, safe at her new husband's side.

Her only regret was that she hadn't been able to have her mother attend. But it was doubtful Mom could have come to any wedding, and they'd agreed to visit her as soon as they got back from their short, thrown-together honeymoon at a nearby mountain lodge.

After dinner, Emily and Dev walked everyone to their cars. Landon was going back to stay with Hayley for tonight, and then he'd spend a couple of days with his friend Chip, whose family lived nearby.

Lady would go on their honeymoon with them, helping Emily with her bridal jitters.

Although she mostly felt happy, not jittery.

They waved to their friends and then turned to each other. The sun set behind the mountains, and Dev pulled her into his arms.

Another kiss, this one just for the two of them. Deeper, lasting longer than the one they'd shared in the church.

"You're sure this was okay?" Dev asked. "You don't feel shortchanged without the big to-do?"

"Not at all. I feel blessed." And as she wrapped her arms around him and laid her head against his strong chest, Emily felt at home.

The sun sent its last rays into the darkening sky, and it felt like a benediction. She couldn't stop the smile from spreading across her face.

There had been darkness, sadness, loss. But it was just as the psalmist said, just as Nate had quoted in their marriage service: *Weeping may endure for a night, but joy cometh in the morning.*

Emily's long time of weeping was past, and she lifted her face to the heavens in thanksgiving.

Now was the season of joy.

* * * * *

*If you enjoyed this K-9 Companions book,
be sure to look for TITLE TK by
Brenda Minton, available May 2022,
wherever Love Inspired books are sold!*

*And don't miss Lee Tobin McClain's latest
full-length romance,* Forever on the Bay,
available May 2022 from HQN Books!

Dear Reader,

I hope you enjoyed escaping to the Rocky Mountains to read *Her Easter Prayer*. I had so much fun writing it! For one thing, the book is set in beautiful Colorado, where I lived for ten years. For another, it's about literacy, a cause very close to my heart. And finally, the book focuses on a very special dog. I'm a major animal lover, and Emily's service dog, Lady, was a joy to create.

Both Emily and Dev have serious issues to overcome, but they manage to do so with the help of faith and friends. And what better time than Easter to focus on redemption, forgiveness and bright tomorrows?

Are you curious about Christine, the Christian singer Emily met, and her handsome bodyguard, Logan? Visit the "extras" section of my website to get a free e-novella about their sweet and romantic love story. You'll need to sign up for my newsletter, but it's quick and easy. And that way, you'll get notice of future books set at the Bright Tomorrows Academy.

I'd love to stay in touch.

Wishing you Easter blessings,
Lee

Get 4 FREE REWARDS!

We'll send you 2 FREE Books plus 2 FREE Mystery Gifts.

Both the **Love Inspired®** and **Love Inspired® Suspense** series feature compelling novels filled with inspirational romance, faith, forgiveness, and hope.

YES! Please send me 2 FREE novels from the Love Inspired or Love Inspired Suspense series and my 2 FREE gifts (gifts are worth about $10 retail). After receiving them, if I don't wish to receive any more books, I can return the shipping statement marked "cancel." If I don't cancel, I will receive 6 brand-new Love Inspired Larger-Print books or Love Inspired Suspense Larger-Print books every month and be billed just $5.99 each in the U.S. or $6.24 each in Canada. That is a savings of at least 17% off the cover price. It's quite a bargain! Shipping and handling is just 50¢ per book in the U.S. and $1.25 per book in Canada.* I understand that accepting the 2 free books and gifts places me under no obligation to buy anything. I can always return a shipment and cancel at any time. The free books and gifts are mine to keep no matter what I decide.

Choose one: ☐ **Love Inspired**
Larger-Print
(122/322 IDN GNWC)

☐ **Love Inspired Suspense**
Larger-Print
(107/307 IDN GNWN)

Name (please print)

Address   Apt. #

City   State/Province   Zip/Postal Code

Email: Please check this box ☐ if you would like to receive newsletters and promotional emails from Harlequin Enterprises ULC and its affiliates. You can unsubscribe anytime.

Mail to the Harlequin Reader Service:
IN U.S.A.: P.O. Box 1341, Buffalo, NY 14240-8531
IN CANADA: P.O. Box 603, Fort Erie, Ontario L2A 5X3

Want to try 2 free books from another series? Call 1-800-873-8635 or visit www.ReaderService.com.

*Terms and prices subject to change without notice. Prices do not include sales taxes, which will be charged (if applicable) based on your state or country of residence. Canadian residents will be charged applicable taxes. Offer not valid in Quebec. This offer is limited to one order per household. Books received may not be as shown. Not valid for current subscribers to the Love Inspired or Love Inspired Suspense series. All orders subject to approval. Credit or debit balances in a customer's account(s) may be offset by any other outstanding balance owed by or to the customer. Please allow 4 to 6 weeks for delivery. Offer available while quantities last.

Your Privacy—Your information is being collected by Harlequin Enterprises ULC, operating as Harlequin Reader Service. For a complete summary of the information we collect, how we use this information and to whom it is disclosed, please visit our privacy notice located at corporate.harlequin.com/privacy-notice. From time to time we may also exchange your personal information with reputable third parties. If you wish to opt out of this sharing of your personal information, please visit readerservice.com/consumerchoice or call 1-800-873-8635. **Notice to California Residents**—Under California law, you have specific rights to control and access your data. For more information on these rights and how to exercise them, visit corporate.harlequin.com/california-privacy.

LIRLIS22

COUNTRY LEGACY COLLECTION

Cowboys, adventure and romance await you in this new collection! Enjoy superb reading all year long with books by bestselling authors like Diana Palmer, Sasha Summers and Marie Ferrarella!

COMING NEXT MONTH FROM
Love Inspired

THE AMISH TWINS NEXT DOOR
Indiana Amish Brides • by Vannetta Chapman

Amish single mom Deborah Mast is determined to raise her seven-year-old twin sons *her* way. But when neighbor Nicholas Stoltzfus takes on the rambunctious boys as apprentices on his farm, she'll learn the value of his help with more than just the children—including how to reopen her heart.

SECRETS IN AN AMISH GARDEN
Amish Seasons • by Lenora Worth

When garden nursery owner Rebecca Eicher hires a new employee, she can't help but notice that Jebediah Martin looks similar to her late fiancé. But when her brother plays matchmaker, Jeb's secret is on the brink of being revealed. Will the truth bring them together or break them apart forever?

EARNING HER TRUST
K-9 Companions • by Brenda Minton

With the help of her service dog, Zeb, Emery Guthrie is finally living a life free from her childhood trauma. Then her high school bully, Beau Wilde, returns to town to care for his best friend's orphaned daughters. Has she healed enough to truly forgive him and let him into her life?

THEIR ALASKAN PAST
Home to Owl Creek • by Belle Calhoune

Opening a dog rescue in Owl Creek, Alaska, is a dream come true for veterinarian Maya Roberts, but the only person she can get to help her run it is her ex-boyfriend Ace Reynolds. When a financial situation forces Ace to accept the position, Maya can't run from her feelings...or the secret of why she ended things.

A NEED TO PROTECT
Widow's Peak Creek • by Susanne Dietze

Dairy shepherdess Clementine Simon's only concern is the safety of her orphaned niece and nephew and *not* the return of her former love Liam Murphy. But could the adventuring globe-trotter be just what she needs to overcome her fears and take another chance on love?

A PROMISE FOR HIS DAUGHTER
by Danielle Thorne

After arriving in Kudzu Creek, contractor and historical preservationist Bradley Ainsworth discovers the two-year-old daughter he never knew about living there with her foster mom, Claire Woodbury. But as they work together updating the house Claire owns, he might find the family he didn't know he was missing...

LOOK FOR THESE AND OTHER LOVE INSPIRED BOOKS WHEREVER BOOKS ARE SOLD, INCLUDING MOST BOOKSTORES, SUPERMARKETS, DISCOUNT STORES AND DRUGSTORES.

LICNM0322